Bad Tickets

Bad Tickets

Kathleen O'Dell

Alfred A. Knopf
New York

I
O'Dell

THIS IS A BORZOI BOOK PUBLISHED BY ALFRED A. KNOPF

Published in the United States by Alfred A. Knopf, an imprint of Random House Children's Books, a division of Random House, Inc., New York.

KNOPF, BORZOI BOOKS, and the colophon are registered trademarks of Random House, Inc.

www.randomhouse.com/teens

Educators and librarians, for a variety of teaching tools, visit us at
www.randomhouse.com/teachers

Library of Congress Cataloging-in-Publication Data
O'Dell, Kathleen.
Bad tickets / Kathleen O'Dell. — 1st ed.
    p.   cm.
SUMMARY: Rebelling against her strict Catholic upbringing in 1967, teenager Mary Margaret sorts through her feelings about her parents and friends, and about sex, while making some decisions about the type of life she wants for herself.
ISBN 978-0-375-83801-9 (trade)
ISBN 978-0-375-93801-6 (lib. bdg.)
[1. Interpersonal relations—Fiction.   2. Conduct of life—Fiction.
3. Catholics—Fiction.   4. Schools—Fiction.   5. High schools—Fiction.
6. United States—History—1961–1969—Fiction.]   I. Title.
PZ7.O2325Bad 2007
[Fic]—dc22
2006003447

Printed in the United States of America

April 2007

10 9 8 7 6 5 4 3 2 1

First Edition

For Mary Shannon,
with gratitude for
thirty years of friendship.
danke schoen,
X.O.

Bad Tickets

1

"Admit it, darling. We've got wicked gorgeous legs," Jane says.

It's a rare and welcome sunny day. My new best friend, Jane, and I are sitting in the alley behind Rexall Drugs with our socks peeled off, trying to tan ourselves on our lunch break. My legs are freckled and milky and dented with elastic marks from my knee-highs. Jane's legs are in another league completely.

"Look here," says Jane, wiggling her toes. "Cutex Wicked White. You want to try it?" She reaches into her black leather bag, takes out the nail polish, and shakes it. "Say yes."

This is Jane's campaign: helping me to choose something outside my usual box of predictables. And I want to, but still I hesitate. "There's no time," I tell her. "My socks will stick."

"Great God, Mary Margaret, I'm just trying to help!"

Jane loves to imitate my mother. Or rather, she imitates

my imitation and exaggerates it. Her eyes twitch. Her hands tremble as if she's fighting her instinct to strangle me. *"Great GOD, Mary Margaret! Pull your dress down! Knees together! Wipe off the lipstick! Spit out the gum! . . ."* Actually, the imitation works as a flash reminder that out of my three, possibly four, attainable futures, there's at least *one* to be avoided at all costs.

I'm still tying my shoes when Jane pushes me off the curb.

"Go!"

We have seven minutes to make it back to Sacred Heart Academy or there will be hell to pay. Jane turns up the transistor radio. Clouds are swelling in the hot blue sky, and cars are zinging past us on Halsey Street. Donovan is singing "Sunshine Superman":

> *Any trick in the book now, baby,*
> *all that I can find. . . .*
> *I'll pick up your hand and slowly blow*
> *your little mind.*

We gallop, tossing our hair and doing the Hitchhike. An old guy in a Ford truck slows down and honks.

"Pervert!" I yell.

"The old ones are *always* perverts," says Jane.

Jane's talking about Avery, her stepfather, who leers at her after too many bourbon and waters. As for Jane's real father, "He's gone" is all she says. I don't know anything else.

We break into a dead sprint until we are panting behind the rusting Cyclone fence at Sacred Heart.

"Cutting it a little close, aren't you?" says my ex-friend Elizabeth Healy.

"Oh really?" says Jane. "Thanks for the observation." Jane calls Elizabeth "She Who Came Before Me." She also likes to say that Elizabeth is notable for her "complete absence of presence."

Elizabeth ignores me altogether and is always a complete snot to Jane. I play at being invisible while they swap insults, though I know Elizabeth is just as disgusted with me.

"How was *lunch*?" asks Elizabeth.

"You would have loved it, Elizabeth," says Jane. "We had soup. Cream of boring. Your favorite."

"Ha," says Elizabeth.

"Oh, I'm sorry," says Jane. "Cream of boring would be too spicy for you, wouldn't it?" Her eyes glaze over. "How about cream of nap, cream of coma, cream of corpse?" She ends in a deep snore.

Elizabeth puts on a phony pout. "Ooh, I'm boring. I want to get knocked up and do time at the House of the Good Shepherd, too!" She stamps her foot. "Boo hoo," she says, wiping an invisible tear.

"I have never been 'knocked up'!" Jane calls after her. "Someone should consult her slang dictionary!" And then to me, softly, "I swear, that girl is going to *die* a virgin."

I laugh at this, but I'm pretty sure that *I'm* going to die a virgin.

Jane and I have special permission to go off campus for lunch because her mother lives just around the corner in this deluxe oasis of new homes rimming the golf course. The thing is, as Elizabeth apparently knows, we roam around instead, playing our music and buying Pixy Stix at Rexall. Lately we've been smoking Kools behind the seventh hole as Jane talks about how in just a month we're going to have our explosive, bombshell-sexy, boom-boom, breakout summer of adventure. It's the kind of talk I never had with Elizabeth. But then, she's changed, too.

Who knows what happened to the sweet, quiet, skinny Elizabeth of my childhood? She seemed to skip directly from "girl life" to being scared and old-ladyish. When she was a kid, I loved her for her ability to sit in one place and focus her attention. She could get lost for hours making an eggshell mosaic. In sixth grade, during spring break, she completed a giant paint-by-numbers copy of a Thomas Gainsborough lady in a feathered hat. Her father framed it in gold and hung it above the stereo. Elizabeth's stuff was not for taping to the refrigerator. I was in awe of her.

But then she got breasts. Big ones. She kept her flat-chested personality and started walking around with her arms crossed all the time. Worst of all, her adored big brother got drafted, and Elizabeth got more and more religious. One day last spring, when we were goofing around in her bedroom, I found this elaborate prayer calendar. She had put a hash mark down for every rosary she said, every mass she attended.

"Jeez, Elizabeth," I said. "It's not a friggin' contest."

She looked at me like I'd slapped her. I felt awful.

"You always make it sound like it's so bad to care about things," she said.

And here I thought I cared way too much about *everything*.

I took a good look at her. Gone was the sweet, quiet self-confidence. She was a worried, lumpy Elizabeth with a prayer calendar. "My Lord," I said, "what happened to you?"

She never answered. I waited. And waited. I asked her, "Are you still my best friend?" Finally she answered, "No."

I went home and sank into a dreary, hopeless funk that dragged on through the summer.

I knew other girls—Constance Cready, Debbie Watts, Kathy McCann—but I've always been a one-best-friend type of person. Some nights I would lie in the dark, feeling my tears crawling into my hair, convinced that I was actually dying of loneliness.

Then Jane happened to me. Now everything's picked up speed. Even the hopeless feeling I get in geometry class is bearable with my brand-new Jane beside me.

"Can we switch pencils?" I whisper. Jane never uses an eraser when she does math. She gives me a brand-new pencil without looking up, just burrowing into this math thing in a way I cannot possibly understand. I lean on my hand and stare at her.

"Miss Hallinan and Miss Stephens." The intercom crackles. "Please see Mother Superior. Miss Hallinan and Miss Stephens. Thank you."

Sister Immaculata looks up from her desk. So does everyone else in class. I'm blushing just picturing Mother Superior dialing the big black office phone with her pale and papery fingers, my mother saying, "What's she done now?" I know I'm in for a scorching afternoon.

But Jane just stands, smooths her skirt, and says, "Shall we?"

As we walk down the hall together, I tell her, "Jane, please. Whatever you do, do not be a smart-ass."

"Me? A smart-ass?"

"Seriously. Once, when we were in second grade, Mother Superior caught Paul Wysocki lying. First she smiled at him, sort of sweet and forgiving. Got him all relaxed. Then she slowly lifted him off the ground using his ears as little handles. It was gruesome."

Mother Superior's office is decorated with file cabinets, a crucifix, and a sunlight-starved philodendron.

"Please sit," she says. We do. She looks at each of us in turn, smiling sweetly, as if she finds us cute as kittens. "So, what did you girls have for lunch today?" she asks.

"Soup!" we say, exactly together. *Ooh, that was good.*

"What kind of soup?"

"Cream of . . . ," I start.

"Broccoli," finishes Jane.

"Really?" says Mother Superior, narrowing her eyes. "And when did you hitchhike down 132nd? Before or after the soup?"

"We did not hitchhike," says Jane.

"Where is your mother, Miss Stephens? I have tried to call her and she's not at home."

6

"I don't know," says Jane.

"And we never see her at mass. My goodness. She must be a very busy woman."

I flick Jane a glance. When she doesn't display the appropriate shame, Mother Superior turns to me.

"Well, Mary Margaret, at least you'll be glad to know I was able to reach *your* mother."

I wince.

Her smile turns acidic. "I told her all about your 'lunch.' Needless to say," Mother says, straightening up in her chair, "your off-campus lunch privileges are now rescinded. In addition, you are to spend the next four weeks lending assistance to the altar guild during lunch hour."

"What does that mean?" asks Jane.

Mother pushes her fingertips together and stares Jane down. "I believe what you meant to say was, 'What does that mean, MOTHER SUPERIOR?' I am not your playground friend."

"I understand . . . *Mother Superior*," says Jane.

Mother glares. "It means that you will polish the pews and clean the confessionals and do anything else Father Dreiser sees fit to ask you. You will come in at eight tomorrow and meet with him."

Just the mention of Father Dreiser produces an immediate stomachache.

"It is my hope," concludes Mother, "that you will *both* come back from the experience with a new humility and an appropriate reverence for the rules of this academy. Good afternoon."

"Thank you, Mother Su-pe-ri-or," we answer in a monotone.

"What a bitch. And we didn't even hitchhike!" says Jane as we head back to class.

"But we did run around at lunch. And we lied about the soup," I say.

"Can you lie about soup? I really don't think that should count," says Jane.

"I'm going to be cooked in a soup," I say. "You know my mother."

"Yes, unfortunately."

Jane says the reason my mother's always angry is she knows she bought a bad ticket. She picked a guy who's not taking her anywhere, so she's been stuck in the same place since 1952. And though I do love my dad, I know Jane's probably right. My mother moved from a house overflowing with crying babies and laundry to her own house full of the same.

And I think that she despises me. She maybe even struggles with it, but who cares? I'll always be the one who showed up uninvited nine months after some parental backseat stuff I really don't want to think about. And I pay for it every day. Believe me.

"Oh my God, Jane," I say, stopping in my tracks. "Aren't you still sort of on probation at this school?"

Jane just smiles. "No one's sending me back to Good Shepherd. In fact, in a couple of weeks, no one will even think about this stuff. Just be cool, okay?"

I look into her eyes. As always, the sharpness there

makes me want to pull myself up. "You're right," I say. "To hell with 'em."

"Okay, then," Jane says. "But I'll tell you what. We can make this fun! I'll trade my diamond tiara for your beanie if we can't do this lunch thing and have a blast." She punches me on the arm. She winks. She sticks out her tongue. She lifts the tip of her nose with her thumb and snorts. "Ya get me?"

I do my Spock. "Well reasoned, Miss Stephens," I say.

And suddenly we are snorting and laughing. I am in big trouble and I am *laughing*. That's my Jane.

2

When I come in the door after school, I usually find my mother, steam iron in hand, banging the wrinkles out of my father's shirts. Not gliding the iron around like the ladies do in commercials. With her, it's *clump huff clump huff*. The steam in the iron sounds exactly like her sighs. Today she's smoking, sorting socks, and watching *Dialing for Dollars*. I walk right up to her and stand between her and the TV.

"I got a call from Mother today," she says, shifting her gaze to a shirt she is folding.

"We were not hitchhiking," I say.

"Oh, of course not," she says. "Know what? Don't go any further." She retrieves her smoldering Pall Mall from the ashtray, takes a drag, and blows a lazy smoke ring. "What do you think is going to happen? That I'm going to take *your* side?"

I'm beginning to get the creeps. She's never this serene.

"I'm not even going to waste my time speaking to you

about this," she says, looking past me to the TV. "Father Dreiser will know what to do."

She is practically silent until dinner. Hardly a word to my father. Usually she's bursting to greet him with the bad news of the day. "Wash your hands!" she shouts. I take my regular seat at the dinette table next to my eleven-year-old sister, Paula.

Mother leads us in saying grace in her slow, deliberate, deeply reverent way. She then gestures to the center of the table and the casserole dish with a big metal serving spoon sticking out of the middle. My dad digs in and dumps the meat-and-rice mixture on his plate. He then helps my littlest sister, who asks, "What's this?"

"It's heart!" says Mother cheerfully.

"Whaddya mean?" asks my brother Kevin.

"It's beef heart!" Mother says. She looks meaningfully at my father. "Only nineteen cents a pound."

My father stops chewing and drops his fork.

"You said to cut down on expenses," Mother says. "And you refuse to take a bag lunch. So instead of giving up my cigarettes as you suggested, I'm going for cheaper cuts." Her smile is overly wide.

"This heart came out of a cow?" asks Paula.

"Yes. Almost the same place steak comes from," says Mother. "Except it's cut out of the chest."

Paula spears a chunk of meat with her fork. "Oh, heart, heart! Oh, bleeding drops of red!" she intones.

"Now THAT'S enough," says my dad.

"And I hope everybody loves it, because there's tons

more in the freezer," says my mom. She takes a big bite and chews like it's filet mignon.

I put my fork in and eat the stuff. It doesn't have much taste. I realize now that the coming storm between my parents has been brewing since yesterday's "budget discussion."

I watch as Kevin carefully picks each chunk of meat from the rice and makes a little pyramid on his plate. My littlest sister, Katie, looks at her plate as her brown eyes brim with tears. "I wish I was Daniel," she says.

"Why's that?" asks my dad.

"Because then I could have a bottle instead." Two perfect little droplets run off her cheeks and into the casserole.

My dad pats Katie on the back. "There, there, Katie-cat. You don't want to be Daniel. You wouldn't be able to stay up and watch *Batman.*"

Katie appears to give this serious thought. "Oh," she says, brightening. "And I wouldn't be in grade two." Katie's always been pretty sensible.

My dad looks down into his food as if he is summoning his courage. Then he looks around the table. "Who likes soy sauce?" he asks.

"Me!" Hands shoot up right and left. Dad goes to the cupboard and pulls out the Chung King. He douses his rice until it's good and inky. He takes a bite. "Mmm," he says. "That ain't bad!"

Kevin grabs the sauce and drowns the little stack of heart parts and tastes them. "Yeah," he says. "It's sort of okay."

"Tastes like meat," says Dad. "Not bad at all!" He beams.

"Yum," says Kevin, forking up another load.

"Let me try!" says Paula.

Dad has gained advantage with nothing but kidlike enthusiasm. Soon all the little kids' plates are swimming in soy sauce. "Hey! Soy sauce tastes good on salad, too!" says Kevin. "Try it, Mary Margaret."

I sneak a look at my mother. Her smug cheerfulness has curdled. I picture a voice bubble over her head: *Curses, foiled again!*

"C'mon!" says Paula. "It's a soy sauce party. You too, Mom!" Paula holds up the bottle of sauce.

My mother does not acknowledge Paula. Instead, she gives Dad her dagger stare. "If only you could take that charm to the bank. We'd all be eating prime rib."

Dad looks down at his plate, chewing innocently.

Mother stands. "I will not go without cigarettes!" She looks up at the ceiling. "Why don't you talk to me?"

"Sorry. I didn't hear a question," says Dad.

"Why does there ALWAYS have to be a QUESTION?"

Katie tries to cover her ears but knocks over her glass of milk instead. She's crying for real now.

I take her plastic cup, set it upright, and start mopping with my napkin. "Shhh, Katie-bug," I say. In my head, I start to clear a mother-free place. *La la la la la la la . . . can't hear you. . . .*

Mother rips off some paper towels, pushes me aside, and takes over cleaning Katie's mess.

"Excuse you," I mumble.

"Oh, now you're getting fresh with me, Mary Margaret?" says Mother. "After hitchhiking during school like a juvenile delinquent . . ."

"You've lost me," says Dad.

"Oh, that's right," says Mother. "You didn't know. But then again, you never asked a QUESTION, because then you might FIND SOMETHING OUT! *Good God!* You might have to be a parent instead of a playmate." She stomps out and heads for their bedroom.

I look my dad straight in the eye. "Where do you get the guts to come home to that every night?"

"Mary Margaret, why don't you and Paula do the dishes?" he says, as if observing me from a great distance.

"All right," I say. "I'll do the stupid dishes. While I hate her!"

"Stop it," says Paula. "Please."

Dad leaves and I'm filling the sink, still steaming.

I hand Paula a wet dish. "She's mental. I wish she'd go out for a pack of her precious Pall Malls and never come back," I say.

"She's my mom and I love her!" Paula says, suddenly defensive.

I put my hand on Paula's head and stare at her pale kid's face. "Paula, you know I'm right about her."

"Well, yeah," she says, "Mom gets mad. But she's already worried about money, and Dad doesn't help when he tries to take away her cigarettes."

"But you hate Mom's cigarettes."

14

"I do. But you know what I mean. Dad doesn't get Mom's feelings. So we have to try harder."

My sister's shoulders are squared, and there is a look of unblinking determination and loyalty in her eyes. Paula's an amazing kid, really.

"Okay, you've made your point. Keep drying," I say.

And so I don't tell her that the only way to survive our mother is to go all dead inside. That I pretend that Mom is screaming behind a wall of thick plate glass. And that even this compromise can leave your heart sore and tired.

3

I wake up extra early the next morning to have some time alone. The house is luxuriously quiet. No one is beating on the bathroom door, no bumping elbows at the breakfast table. Still in my pj's, I stir up a glass of Tang and head out to our skinny side yard, where a bunch of neglected roses are now blooming.

No one ever comes out here but me. There's a little rusty Crisco can I hide by the gutter for my cigarette butts. I'll sit and stare at the yellow and red blooms until they turn all glowy. The yelling and the kitchen's crash banging and the TV noise become a sort of distant buzz. I'll think, *Remember when I lived in the crazy crowded house with my insane mother and forty-nine siblings? Sooo long ago . . .*

This morning in the dead quiet, with my bare feet on the dirt and my face turned toward the sun, I feel like one of the roses myself. I almost forget that I'm scheduled for a meeting with Father Dreiser. Out of habit or instinct, I send up a prayer to the Virgin, pleading for merciful treatment. *I wish I could just go to your cloud instead*, I tell her. I mean it.

So I believe it's not entirely a coincidence when I see a smiling Jane waiting for me when I get to the rectory. "Guess what?" she says. "Father Dreiser has a funeral this morning!"

"Cool!" I say. "What do we do?"

"They said we could see Father Waters at eight-fifteen instead," says Jane.

"Glory be to God!" I say. Father Waters is young and sweet and popular and kind of handsome, too. When our class goes to confession, the nuns have us count off before lining up at the confessionals. Otherwise, given a choice, no kid would ever go to Father Dreiser, and Father Waters's line would be a mile long. He seems happy to let me off with a Hail Mary and always says hi to me on the playground.

"Good morning, you two," says Father Waters. He looks up at the sky, shading his eyes.

"Good morning, Father," we chorus. He surprises us, coming outside like this.

"Why don't we have a seat right here? It seems we have a few minutes of sunshine, and I don't want to waste them."

Father sits at the top of the steps. Jane and I sit below him. It's weird having an up-close view of his fallen-down sock and an inch of hairy man leg. You forget priests have man legs, you know?

"Why in the world would you girls hitchhike?" he asks.

"Oh, but we didn't," says Jane.

"We were dancing, actually," I say, trying to sound natural.

17

"On 132nd?" asks Father.

"We went to Rexall for candy and sort of danced back to school," says Jane. "And I *know* it sounds ridiculous," she adds.

"You can't leave school at lunch anymore," says Father.

We say we know. We both nod in agreement, trying to show how sincerely we accept our punishment. "And we know we have to clean the church," says Jane.

"Good," says Father, clapping his hands on his knees. "Did I ever tell you girls about the time I spent hitchhiking before I went to seminary? I was searching around, trying to make up my mind. I was something of a dharma bum. Or at least I tried to be."

We look at him blankly. *A darn bum?*

"Kerouac?" says Father Waters, waving his hand in front of our faces. "Oh, well, you girls should read him. In a year or two, perhaps. He was a Catholic boy, you know."

For a moment, I think Father Waters looks a little sad, like he's seeing something inside himself. *You too?* I want to say.

"Just check in with Mrs. Demetrio at lunch," he says, smiling again, "and she'll tell you what to do." He stands and places a hand on each of our shoulders. "I don't expect that you'll be doing anything like this again soon."

We shake our heads and promise.

"God," says Jane as Father walks back inside. "He's so . . . *normal*. Why couldn't my mother have married some guy like that?"

"Because he's a priest?" I suggest.

18

"I'd take a priest over AVERY any day."

Jane never pronounces her stepfather's name without rolling her eyes. He officially adopted her and everything, but there's no father-daughter love lost between those two. In any case, I do understand why she likes Father Waters. He makes you feel privileged to have him like you.

On our first day cleaning, we get keys to all the secret rooms in the church from the rectory secretary. To my eyes, Sacred Heart Church is so modern, it could pass for a giant living room almost. The altar has been turned around and no one speaks Latin here anymore: all part of the church's effort to explain itself to us, the "now" people of 1967. But when I show Jane around, the place's mystery and strangeness again seem as ancient as the lingering smells of burning beeswax and incense.

It's strangely fun running in church, breaking into the places girls usually can't go, like the room behind the sacristy where the priests keep their vestments. I'm fingering all the silk and linen when I hear Jane groan.

She's standing just outside, face to face with a statue of Jesus. His robe is open and he points to his bloody, thorn-pricked heart. Jane pokes at the holes of the statue's hands. She's trembling.

"Ugh. So much hopeless freakin' bloodshed. Doesn't it make you want to puke?"

"Actually, no," I say.

"But why?" she asks.

"Well, when you're raised like me, six masses a week since first grade, you're just used to it."

"It's the worst sort of brainwashing, Mary Margaret. The blood." She shudders, turns her back on the statue. "Disgusting. I refuse to look at it for another second."

I sense not to probe further.

One of our jobs is to dust and carpet-sweep inside the confessionals, so we prop open every door with a missal. Never have I seen these boxes open in broad daylight.

"You rang?" says Jane. Suddenly she's peeking at me through the priest's side of the confessional wall.

"Father Jane! You scared me!"

"Man, it is weird in here," she says. "I've got a little door and everything."

The outline of her head appears and disappears through the golden screen as she opens and shuts the little door. She holds her hand up and blesses me: "Go, and sin some more!"

She shuts the door. I hear her galloping toward the altar. When I step out, I see she's opened the silky box that holds the chalice. She picks through a baby blue box and holds up a host.

"Put that back," I say.

"Why?" Jane looks down into the box with its rows of snowy white wafers. To her, they could have been any old crackers.

"You're not supposed to touch those," I say.

"But it's not communion *yet*," says Jane. "Isn't it still, like, bread?"

"I don't care," I say. "I just don't feel . . . right."

"Mary Margaret!" says Jane, surprised. "You're turning pale."

"Uh, please. Could you just be a friend and put it back?"

"All right," she sighs. "You and your church stuff. Sheesh! It's all such a big secret. Everything's hidden in a box or a pocket or under glass. No touching! What's the big deal?" She puts the lid down on the box. "I hate seeing you turn all uptight."

"Do NOT call me uptight," I say. "*Elizabeth* is uptight."

Jane nods. "Well, you're right about that."

"Let's eat," I say.

We have five minutes to stuff down a sandwich before returning to class. We kneel in the choir loft and spy on everyone on the playground.

"See? Isn't this nice?" asks Jane. "Better than eating at our desks."

"Yep."

She cups her hands around her eyes. "Let's look for practice boys."

"Huh?"

"Practice boys for summer." She taps the glass. "Anyone make-outable. Pick one."

"I can't even imagine," I say. Which is true. There is one sophomore boy who interests me. Actually, both Elizabeth and I had huge secret crushes on him. He's almost six-four and has reddish blond hair, a beautiful jaw, and skin that looks permanently sunburned. After a bout with polio when he was seven, he never fully recovered the use of his left leg. He's the youngest of four tough boys in a family of athletes. He's bitter and sarcastic, and his name is Mitchell Dunn. He scares me.

21

"We need more eligible bachelors," says Jane. "Some decent tickets."

"Um, how about Mitchell Dunn?" I say casually.

"Don't know him," Jane says. "Unless you're talking about the limpy guy." She stops. "Him?"

"Sort of always thought he was kind of cute," I say.

"Yes, sweetie, but is he a *ticket?*" asks Jane. "I do understand the impulse, but we're not on a rescue mission."

It's a cruel thing to say, but I just shrug. For Jane, Mitch is not an obvious choice boyfriendwise. All I know is that for me, Mitchell sightings carry their own sick electricity. If I'm in a crowd, I tune in until I can pick up the thrilling frequency of his hard, nasal voice. When my mother drives past his house to the 88-Cent Store, I pinch my thigh to make myself sit still while squinting into his picture window. I wonder if Elizabeth still dreams about him.

"Let me think about it," I say.

"No fair," says Jane. "Because now you won't even let me say *uptight.*"

"I know, I know," I say. "Maybe I need more practice at being spontaneous."

"No comment," says Jane.

4

By the time school's over, the promising morning sunshine has been extinguished by heavy storm clouds.

"Shoot," I say, shoving my books underneath my coat. The gutters are clogged, and rain plunges over the roof like a waterfall. I'm going to have to take a bucketful down the neck. I flip up my collar, hunker down, and leap, and I'm immediately drenched.

"See you at home!" yells Paula. She's pulling little Katie by the hand and straggling to keep up with Kevin. Their Hush Puppies are already dark with water.

"See you, Paula!" I yell. I watch them splash their way through the crosswalk. I can feel my books slipping and stop to heave them before they fall into some puddle. I jerk up my knee until I get hold of the bottom of the load, then pull the books over my chest. In the process, I elbow someone next to me.

"Sorry," I say.

"It's okay," says Elizabeth. She is completely buttoned up in a plastic raincoat and standing under a huge black umbrella. Of course, her books are bundled in a waterproof canvas bag—with a zipper.

I'm antsy standing here with her, side by side, waiting for the walk light. This fakey thing we've got into—pretending we were never close as sisters—feels awful. As soon as I can, I scramble until I'm a good five yards ahead. I struggle to keep my balance and my dignity as I trudge through wet gravel with rain coursing down the ends of my bangs and into my eyes. She follows me like a ghost—a dry, well-organized ghost with a book bag—for the next four blocks. For once, it feels good to turn away onto my street.

"BATHROOM!" my mother shrieks when I come in the door. "This floor has just been waxed." She huffs as she puts down a beach towel for us to drip on. "Everything in the tub!" she says.

I try to push past her, but she grabs my shoulder. "Heavens. Go and get a washrag. You have mascara running down your face."

"It was raining, Mother."

"You wear too much makeup," she declares. "Don't cheapen yourself."

I grit my teeth and march to the bathroom. No sooner do I begin blotting my face than Mother sticks her head in the door.

"Another thing, Mary Margaret," she says. "It is still your

job to make sure all the kids clean their lunch pails, in case you've forgotten."

"Fine, Mother."

I join Paula and Kevin at the kitchen trash can. We jostle each other trying to dump the garbage from our lunch pails at the same time. My stuff falls in last and Paula gasps. "Oh, Mary Margaret!" she whispers.

"What?" I look down. There, on a crumpled paper towel, lies a communion wafer.

"Shhh!" I say. I give Paula one of those looks that lets her know I'll sock her. I pluck the wafer off the paper and run to the bathroom.

I hold the wafer up to the light above the sink. It is embossed with the letters IHS. I run my finger around its delicate edge, so thin and sharp. I hear Jane in my head saying: *Go on! Eat it!*

Everyone knows no one is ever supposed to touch communion with anything but the tongue. Altar boys hold a golden plate under your chin at communion in case the wafer should fall. And even though this is an unblessed wafer, I can't believe I'm in my own bathroom with my hands all over this almost sacred thing.

Knock knock knock. "I need the Desitin!" says my mother.

"Just a sec." I flush the empty toilet to make a sound, stick the wafer in my mouth, cross myself, and make my own unholy communion. I'm now Jane's official sister in the Church of Sin.

My baby brother is whimpering. I open the door. There's

Mother with sleepy Daniel on her hip. She gives me a quick look up and down.

"Mary Margaret, you roll down that skirt," she says sharply.

I silently hand her the ointment and watch them go down the hall toward her bedroom, Daniel's chubby arm around my mother's back. She absentmindedly kisses him on the head, and I wonder, *Was I ever that easy to love?*

"I'm in love," says Jane.

"No, you're not," I say.

"Well, I wish I was," says Jane. She's sitting cross-legged in the grass in her pegged jeans and moccasins, making a daisy chain.

Who would be eligible for Jane? With her horsetail-thick, honey-colored hair and enormous blue eyes, she seems to be the kind of girl boys would line up for. She might be the prettiest girl in the school, but I don't know if the boys are catching on to this. My theory is: boys are scared of girls who aren't scared. And Jane is fearless. I almost think she might look good in armor. In fact, she would look *fabulous* in armor.

"What do you think about the Shea brothers?" asks Jane.

"What about 'em?"

"What if I asked them both over for a swim?"

"You want both of them?" I ask.

"Yeah," says Jane. "One for you and one for me!"

"No, no, and no."

Jane lowers her chin and looks into my eyes. She lifts her

chain of daisies and places it on my head like a crown. "Mary Margaret, let me decorate you," she says. She opens her hand and fills it with little white flowers. She slips the stems in the buttonholes of my blouse and behind my ears. I'm about to shake the blossoms off like a wet dog when she stops me short.

"Don't you dare move," she says. She stands and snaps a big wand of yellow forsythia from a bush. "You need a scepter," she says. She places the branch in my hand, stands back, folds her arms, and smiles. "See, you're a flower queen," she says. "You are the beautiful queen fairy."

She loves to do this to me—pretend that I'm beautiful, that we both are beauties together. I used to wonder if she was making fun of me and hid my body or turned my face. But now I know that isn't it. And now I'm trying to see what Jane sees and not be afraid of it.

I take a deep breath. "All right. Invite the brothers Shea," I say. "And hurry before I change my mind."

5

True to her word, that Friday, Jane invites the boys over after school. In a stroke of luck, not only do we have sunshine, but her mother is out shopping.

"We will have the boys all to ourselves," Jane says.

I look at myself in my gingham-check bikini. It's bad enough here in Jane's bedroom, but when the sunlight hits this Irish-white skin of mine, I'm going to give off a blinding glare. I watch as Jane strips off her wool skirt and tosses it on the bed. She's wearing zebra-print underwear.

Where do you get those? What would my mother think? What would Paula and Kevin say when they saw those things in the laundry basket? Or—yipes!—my father?

In my house, all the woman stuff is top-secret. My mom whispered when she handed over the Kotex, the garter belt, the training bra. You whispered about it, put on the gear, and then pretended nothing was ever said.

Jane has her own room with a big double bed and baby pink carpeting. I never have her over at my house. For one thing, we wouldn't have a private moment. For another, my thing with Jane is all mine. I don't want her to be part of my world with the mess and chaos and yelling. So we hole up here, listening to her hi-fi and her magnificent scratchless record albums while her mother and stepfather sip cocktails. For me, it is heaven.

"You look very Brigitte Bardot," says Jane, fastening the top of her white bikini.

"No. *You* look very Brigitte Bardot," I say. "I look very Casper."

"I bet bachelor number two will tell you different," she says.

"You mean Tommy?" Tommy Shea has a habit of bouncing up on his toes when he talks and kind of leaning into a conversation. He's always borrowing things from me: nickels for the milk line, Pink Pearl erasers. "He's eager, yeah. But I never sensed anything . . . romantic."

"You know what John said when I asked him over? He asked if my parents were 'loaded'! Just because we have a pool." Jane wrinkles her nose. "I mean, he's cute and a senior, but I hope he's not a big retard."

Tommy is our age, and I just expect him to be a retard. All the boys in our class are.

The doorbell rings with a fancy-sounding chime. It is the perfect doorbell for this house, with its ivory French provincial furniture and twinkly chandeliers. My first thought

29

when I saw the house was you knew nobody here ever canned their own green beans. Everything is store-bought, all the way.

Tommy is impressed and looks out of place in his wrinkled T-shirt and rubber thongs. I sort of feel for him. He keeps turning his head around and gawking. "Wow," he says.

John concentrates on Jane. "So, Stephens, where's the pool?" he asks.

"Through here." Jane leads us down the hall to the living room.

There, framed in the floor-to-ceiling window, is a shimmering turquoise pool, kidney-shaped and surrounded by Japanese-looking shrubbery. Jane opens a sliding door and steps into the sunlight. "Wow," says Tommy.

"Come on out," Jane says.

Tommy immediately runs and starts bouncing on the diving board. When he's jumped as high as he can, he grabs his knees, hollers, and plunges like a cannonball into the water. The rest of us catch the splash. "Hey, it's freezing in here!" he yells.

"You'll get used to it," Jane says.

"Maybe," says John. "But you're gonna get used to it first!" He swoops Jane up in his arms and heaves her into the pool. She rises to the surface, sputtering. I stand with my arms wrapped around my waist. How mortifying to think of muscly, bare-chested John Shea picking me up next. To my relief, he completely ignores me and jumps in with the others.

I watch as John repeatedly dives deep and grabs Jane by

the ankle. She disappears beneath the water and comes up gasping. Tommy circles, laughing. I have the feeling that both boys want nothing more than to perpetually fondle Jane's legs and ankles. She is the boy magnet, the mermaid. I wonder if anyone would notice if I slipped away to sit and watch her giant color TV.

"Hey, Mary Margaret," calls Tommy. "Are you gonna jump in, or are you a coward?"

"The second thing," I say.

"Do I have to get out and push you in?" he asks.

I sit and dangle my legs in the cool water. I'm covered in goose bumps.

"How come," Tommy says, making small talk, "you don't hang out with Elizabeth Healy anymore?"

"Did you say Healy?" shouts John. "Dave's little sister?"

"Yeah," Tommy says. "Why?"

"Man, what happened to *her*, anyway?" John asks. "Suddenly she's built like a brick shit house."

"If she heard you say that, she would commit suicide," I say. Jane turns abruptly and gives me a burning look.

I'm flustered. *What'd I say?*

I disappear underwater and try to adjust my eyes to the sear of the chlorine. Tommy comes down to join me, his brown hair waving like seaweed, little bubbles coming out of his nose. He starts gargling a song and gesturing like an opera singer, but I can't make out the tune.

"What was that?" I ask when we come up.

"Guess," he says. "Try it again."

We both go under, and Tommy creeps closer to my ear this time. I get it! "Everyone loves the king of the sea! Right?"

He pushes his wet hair out of his eyes. "Yeah. *Flipper*," he says. "Now it's your turn."

I duck under and try the theme song to *The Flintstones,* which he gets right away. We go back and forth like that for a while, with him singing and me shouting, until suddenly, in the middle of me shouting "*Mr. Ed!*" I see his pale bluish face swim up to mine. And he kisses me.

This is my first boy kiss, underwater or otherwise. We stand up and look at each other face to face. And then we go under again.

I run my hands over Tommy's back. His skin seems extraordinarily slick. He presses his face to mine and pushes the tip of his tongue between my lips. I think I might lose consciousness. The kisses are so soft and thrilling. We dunk under about three or four more times, and each time the kisses get a little bolder and I get a little dizzier. After a really passionate kiss, I start to feel like, *What am I doing with Tommy Shea?* I wiggle free and swim underwater until I reach the other edge of the pool. Then I see Jane is already out. And she's . . . topless.

"Aw," says John, dangling her bikini top above the water. "Don't you want it back?"

"Well, *yes*, John," says Jane. "But I'm not going to drown for it."

"Come back in!" he demands.

"No thanks," Jane says. "I think I'll stay high and dry for

a while." She walks back to the sliding glass door and pulls out her straw beach bag. She lights a cigarette, her breasts still bared to the sun, and saunters over to the diving board, where she sits, paying no particular attention to anyone.

Tommy's gaze is exceptionally bloodshot. Suddenly he totally repulses me.

To Jane, this is a game of chicken. I climb the ladder out of the water, grab a towel, and drape it over her shoulders because she's not going to do it on her own.

"BOOOOOO!" bellows John through megaphone hands.

"Thanks, sweetie," murmurs Jane.

John is at a loss all by himself. He drags his wet body from the pool and sits on the cement with a spanking sound. He swings his head to get his long, damp bangs out of his eyes and reaches over with his drippy hand to pick up Jane's pack of Kools. "Ha!" he laughs, pointing at Jane. "That's a *Negro* cigarette."

"Really?" says Jane, all fake fascination. "And which Negro told you that?"

"Our dad works with them," volunteers Tommy. "In Albina."

"No," John corrects him. "They work FOR my dad. At the cleaners."

Jane remains motionless for a few moments, looking at John in silence. And then, as if rousing herself from a dream, she hits herself on the forehead and looks down at her invisible wristwatch. "Jesus, look at the time!" she says. "I had no idea."

"What?" John looks over either shoulder as Jane scrambles around the edges of the pool, frantically picking up towels.

"My piano teacher will be here in minutes. And my mother. And I'm not dressed and I haven't practiced. . . ." Jane drops a towel over John's head. "Come on, everybody!" she says. "Out, out, out!"

I see John looking at her with narrowed eyes, while Tommy's just confused. But as soon as our towels are tied around our waists, Tommy takes my hand. And he won't let it go. As we follow Jane back through the house to the front door, he swings my arm back and forth. And he keeps on squeezing!

I'm completely queasy. I feel like he's married me without my permission. Will he be following me, trying to hold my hand at school? Shit.

Jane holds the door open. John leaves without a word, but Tommy, still holding my hand, pulls me outside with him. "Goodbye, Mary Margaret," he whispers in a tone I don't want to hear, as if he wants something soft back from me. He leans forward to kiss me again. I turn my cheek. It's a crappy thing to do. "Okay, bye," I tell him. I can't look him in the eye, so I turn to the house and shut the door.

"Do you think they even noticed that I don't have a piano?" asks Jane.

I don't say anything.

"What happened out there?" Jane asks. "You look sick."

My eyes are stinging with tears and I can't stop them. I shake my head and wipe my cheeks. "I don't want a boy to be in love with me," I say so fiercely, I surprise myself.

Jane puts an arm around my shoulders. "Oh, Mary Margaret," she says. "Just because he loves you doesn't mean you

34

have to love him back." She smiles and pats me gently. "He's just practice, like I said."

Easy for you, I think. "How do you do it?" I ask her. "How do you make all this boy stuff feel completely weightless?"

"I have a heart of stone, that's how," she says. "Listen, I'll pour you a vodka and Tab, we'll lay out. By the time you go home, you'll have a tan stomach *and* you won't give a shit. Things aren't so difficult, I promise."

6

The next day, after I observe my parents all morning, it hits me why I'm so miserable at romance. I inherited it from *them*. It's their wedding anniversary, and they're supposed to celebrate, yet they have absolutely no idea how to do such a thing. As a matter of fact, no one would have mentioned the anniversary if Paula hadn't brought it up.

"Why don't you let me take you out for steak, Cynthia?" my dad says after an endless silence.

"Because we can't afford it and I don't have anything nice to wear," she grumbles.

"We'll splurge," says Dad. "Why don't you go over to Betty's and see if she has a dress to borrow?"

Mother looks stung. Aunt Betty's heavy in the hips, and I'll bet she's thinking my father has just pointed out how much weight she's gained.

"I don't know. I'd need to get my hair done. . . ."

I can feel my lip curling. I've known for almost two years

that my mom and dad got married because of me, that the anniversary date is a fake-out for everyone who likes to count backward from my birthday to their wedding day. Of course, all the relatives already know. I'd say something right now, but God—poor Paula. She probably believes that babies are placed in their mothers' bellies by fairies.

Finally, Dad volunteers to take all of us kids out for the day. My mother will have all afternoon to get the dress and do her hair and take a bubble bath if she wants. She shoots him a look about the bubble bath remark.

"Sure," she says. "Will you scrub the tub before you go?"

"We will!" says Paula, thrilled that there's some attempted romance in the house. My little sister is forever trying to spice up everyone's lives by doing fifth-grade stuff like putting blue food coloring in our water glasses or spraying Tinkerbell eau de cologne on the lightbulbs. She lives in a land of hope and innocent assumptions—a place I left behind. But still, I want her to stay as long as she can.

After Paula finishes in the bathroom, we all pile in the station wagon. Dad brings the diaper bag and some crackers, bananas, and formula. We stop at Piggly Wiggly and buy a six-pack of Nehi strawberry pop and a bag of Fritos, then speed down Marine Drive along the muggy Sandy River. Near the airport, we park on the gravel shoulder and my dad lets us sit on the roof of the car. We hang out for at least an hour, watching the planes take off. Dad and Kevin hang together, pointing at the sky and talking about jets. Me, Paula, and Katie play patty-cake with Daniel and try bouncing him around so he won't get cranky.

"Maybe it's time to take Danny somewhere else," Paula says.

"You think so?" Dad shades his eyes.

"We haven't even seen one good landing yet," Kevin says.

"I know, but Danny needs to run around a little," I say.

"707!" says Dad. "There, to the east. It's coming in!"

"Hey!" says Kevin.

I can feel the ground rumble as the jet blisters the air. Daniel's body stiffens, and I clap my hand against his ear and hold his head to my chest.

"Aaaaaaaaaaaahh!" screams Kevin. My dad yells, too, lifting his hands to the sky. It appears they can almost touch the rivets on the belly of the plane as it bears down overhead, out thundering all their hollering. When the jet finally lands and rolls along the runway, the only sound left is Daniel's jangled, screaming sobs.

"He's scared to death!" I yank the sleeve of my father's shirt. "We have to leave," I say. "Right NOW!"

I don't realize how angry I sound until I see my dad's face. Dear Jesus, I sound exactly like my mother. Kevin stands beside him with his arms folded, smirking.

"I'm sorry, Dad," I say, quickly trying to sound like myself again. Daniel is still sobbing into my neck. "I just think maybe we should take him to the park."

My dad looks at Daniel shaking and reaches out to stroke his hair, as if he can hear the cries for the first time. "Okay, yeah," he says. "Maybe we should."

"Fun killer," says Kevin as he walks back to the car.

At the park, Dad and Kevin throw a baseball back and forth while it's left to Paula and Katie and me—the girls' team—to chase Daniel around and make sure he doesn't eat dirt or fall down or get hit on the head with anything. I'm about two feet from them when a stupid Frisbee whizzes inches over Daniel's ear before crashing into the swing set. I'm furious and can hardly wait to find the jerk so I can fling it back at his stupid head.

"Over here!"

Before I even know who's where, I throw recklessly, focusing just in time to see the Frisbee turn vertical and smash Mitchell Dunn right in the mouth. He's all of eight feet away and doesn't have a chance to duck. He puts his hand to his lips and looks down at his fingers. Blood.

God help me. I pick up Daniel and rush toward him.

"Now you've upset me," he says evenly.

"Shoot. Shoot," I say. "You're bleeding."

He holds up a blood-smudged finger. "So it appears."

"I'm sorry. I'm just so . . . sorry."

His watery blue eyes burn through me. And then there's that chafed and angry skin on his face—made a little angrier by shaving. I flinch and wait for him to yell at me. Instead, he points to his dog. "You think you're stupid? Don't ever get a damn cocker spaniel," he says. He bends down and politely covers the dog's ears. "They're the stupidest," he whispers. The dog pants and smiles up at me, oblivious. I have to laugh.

He squints, pointing to Daniel. "So, he yours? I didn't know you had kids."

39

I shift the baby to my other hip. "Yeah, well, there's a lot of things you don't know about me."

"Oh yeah?" he says. "Actually, I do know some *stuff*."

"What *stuff*?" I ask.

"Stuff," he says, looking me up and down. "And let's leave it at *that*."

He yanks at his dog's collar, starts limp-walking backward, the dog following, and lifts his hand. "So long, then," he says. I think Mitchell Dunn might be smiling at me, but not quite? I spend the rest of the day trying to figure out exactly what stuff he could possibly be talking about. Is this good or bad?

7

"Such a relief to hear your mother survived her night out on the town," says Jane on Monday morning. She runs some pale lipstick around her mouth, looks in the mirror, and smacks her lips.

"Make that a night out on 182nd," I say.

"It's sort of tragic, don't you think? Your parents, stuck together in eternal low expectations." She hands me some blush. I take out the fluffy brush, rub it in the pink powder, then click the compact shut.

"Oh, why even bother?" I say. "It's useless."

Jane grabs the blush from my hand, opens it, and begins sweeping my cheeks with the brush. "You must ALWAYS bother," Jane says. "People who don't bother grow up to eat steak once a year on 182nd."

I'm quiet. Though true, this stings.

"Oh, that was awful of me, wasn't it?" says Jane.

"Look," I say. "It isn't the first time you've referred to my

41

father's 'bad tickethood.' And we know my mother's hope-less. It's not like I can disagree."

"No. Really. That was really crummy. Forgive me, I beg of you."

"Drop it. It's okay." I turn to leave the bathroom, expect-ing Jane to just follow. Instead, she stands square in front of me.

"Mary Margaret," she says. "Please. Please listen to me."

I do listen, because Jane has suddenly lost all her poise. I've never seen that before.

"You are a fabulous person. And you are my best, best friend. I really want to . . . *deserve* you," she says. "Do you un-derstand that?"

"Uh, sure."

"Good," she says. And then she hugs me tight. Sort of too tight, I think. And then I feel a little concerned and hug her back.

I've never told Jane what I think of *her* mother. Or what my mother thinks about her mother. The first time they met, my mother had dropped by Jane's to pick me up for a dental appointment. Mrs. Stephens, in all her lacquered cheerfulness, swooped down on her and leaned through the car window and let loose with a breathless, one-sided conversation.

"Oh, you are so smart!" she said.

"Pardon me?" said my mother.

"Avery and I would have moved out here *years* ago if we'd known. You get so much for your dollar, don't you?" said

Barbara Stephens, nodding yes to her own question. "Compared to Southwest Portland, I mean."

"Well, yes," my mother said coolly. "Compared to Southwest, I suppose."

"And you have garage space and parking and everything is *so much* easier. It's absolutely lovely. But the *shopping* . . ." She lifted an eyebrow.

My mother gazed at her uncomprehendingly.

"Well, you can always go downtown, can't you? If you need something better."

"Uh-huh," said my mother.

"Anyway, the children here are, in general, well behaved. Not so . . . spoiled? Much nicer girls, which was the point of moving."

I prayed that Mrs. Stephens would say nothing about Jane and House of the Good Shepherd, because my mother would've separated us for good. Luckily, Mrs. Stephens's babbling took another turn.

"I tell Jane, 'To those who much is given much is expected.' But there's no substitute for having to struggle a bit and do without. I'm not talking wrong-side-of-the-tracks going without. Just a wholesome mix, that's all." She caught her breath. "You sure you don't have time for coffee?"

"I'm running oh so late," said my mother.

"Oh! And that's another thing. There's no traffic, really. I don't think I've been late for an appointment since we moved in. And I'm *always* late for appointments. . . ."

When Mrs. Stephens finally released us and we were free

to back out of the driveway, my mother muttered, "Well, that explains everything."

"What do you mean?" I asked.

"If Jane isn't careful . . . ," my mother said, pausing as if she didn't have to finish the sentence.

"What?"

My mother sighed. "If Jane isn't careful, she's going to grow up to be a very *silly* girl."

Now, I actually agreed with my mother about Mrs. Stephens. But I knew enough to guess that *silly*, in this sentence, was supposed to be just loaded with extra meaning. I didn't ask about it, though. I satisfied myself with thinking that if my mother were just a little more *silly*, maybe she'd have friends other than her sisters. My mother could have used a Jane.

"Are you ready to emerge?" Jane asks after our bathroom hug.

"I'm blushed and lipsticked," I say.

I set foot outside and I bump right into Tommy Shea.

The halls are crowded. I stuff down all my embarrassment. Tommy looks me in the face for a total of one second, then walks by without a word. He isn't exactly cool about it. Actually, he's sort of jittery?

"I guess it's worse for him than it is for you," says Jane.

"No, it isn't," I say. I've started to plan what to say to him the next time I see him when the clique of junior and senior boys who hang out by the big double doors burst into applause. I spin around, thinking I'll find someone who dropped their books or something. But they're applauding Jane and me!

"What?" I ask.

Several boys laugh and lean back. "*What?*" says Jerry Conrad in a mincing little imitation. They all laugh again.

Jane pinches the sleeve of my sweater and says, "Let's go." We go only five feet before a voice booms in a deep, dirty bass:

> *"Hey there Little Red Riding Hood,*
> *You sure are lookin' good . . .*
> *You're everything a big bad wolf would*
>   *want."*

"Don't look back," says Jane. But I can't help it. Everyone is looking at us. Their jeering makes me want to throw something, make them stop.

"Knock it off, you jackasses!" I yell.

The whole stupid pack lift their heads and wail, "Aarooooooooooh!" John Shea is smack in the middle, laughing the hardest of them all.

"Mary Margaret, boys are simply stupid," Jane says. "Keep walking."

I do what she says, but I don't get it. She doesn't seem embarrassed in the least. Her chin is held high and there's a little extra swish in her hips. I get moving and manage to keep my mouth shut until we're seated in English class. "Do you know what's going on?" I ask Jane.

Then, out of the corner of my eye, I see Constance Cready nudge Kathy McCann.

"All right. What do you guys know?" I ask them.

Constance sets her jaw. "Do not ask me," she says prissily. Kathy chews the inside of her lip and stares into space as if to say, *Who's talking?*

Suddenly I'm almost light-headed with hurt. I remember when Connie's front tooth got knocked out during first-grade recess and I gave her my little chapel veil to bleed on. Kathy's dad and mine have been fishing buddies for years. How could these girls cut me, just like that?

Jane fixes me with her firm, phony smile until I smile back in the exact same way. "Okay, that's better," she says. Then she turns around and ignores me. I still have the smile on.

"Jane," I whisper, hating my desperate-sounding voice.

She turns around, squeezes my hand, and says, "Next period. Lunch. Church."

Yes, just twenty minutes from now. We can go out the back of the building and avoid the lunch crowd. I hold that thought until the *brrrrring!*

"God, I thought you were going to fall apart," says Jane as soon as the vestibule doors close behind us. "It doesn't behoove you."

"Well, what *would* behoove me?"

"Let's sit," she says. "Okay. The first thing you do—the very first thing when people ambush you for any reason—is . . . *stick a pin in the map.*"

"Meaning?"

"Look around, make a note of where you are. Don't go charging ahead. You'll just get lost."

"Okay," I say.

"It's what generals do. What would have happened to Napoleon if he just had a hissy fit and started firing in confusion every time someone snuck up on his troops?"

"He'd get shot," I say.

"Exactly. You have to have a plan, Mary Margaret. Whenever you don't know what's going on, don't start talking or fighting or crying. Just stick a pin in the map. Figure out where you are, and where your enemies are, before you come back at them." She raises her hand as if taking an oath. "I guarantee this works with parents and teachers and boys. *Anybody* who tries to pull the rug out from under you."

Jane motions me closer. "Did I ever tell you about the time my mother caught me on the phone at three a.m.? This is weeks before I tried to run away with Roger. I was in my nightie and breathing heavy into the receiver, saying things to this boy that would make *any* mother croak, when I sense her right behind me."

"How horrible!"

"Anyway, I didn't freak out. I stopped for a second, pressed down the cradle slooooooowly, and then started talking absolute nonsense." Jane goes glassy-eyed. "GRAMMA, HELLO? I GIVE MICKEY MOUSE THREE MIDNIGHT COOKIES. . . ." She laughs. "Or something like that. My mom takes the phone from my hand, and of course there's nothing but dial tone. Anyway, she ended up leading me back to my bed, sure I was sleepwalking."

I love when she tells me stuff like this, gives me clues for how to revel in the most awful moments. "There is just nobody like you," I say.

"Or you," she says. "Believe me. We will be VICTORI-OUS. Whatever the hell is going on." She turns to the life-size statue of the Virgin Mary behind us. "Sorry. I meant *heck*," she says, and crosses herself.

Mary is standing with her arms outstretched, her eyes downcast, smiling in her *Mona Lisa* way. A serpent hisses beneath her sandaled feet. And I realize for the first time that Mary was a *girl*. Not just a heavenly sort of mom from a fairy tale, but a girl—like me. Why am I thinking this? Maybe it is because this particular statue makes her look so young. And I like the relaxed way she is standing on the serpent, almost as if to say, *Oh, brother.*

"So think," Jane says. "A plan of attack. . . ." She rests her chin in her hand, drums her cheek with her fingers.

I watch her awhile, then a lightbulb goes on. "Jane," I say, lighter and happier than I ever expected to be. "I know where to start. I know where to stick the pin!"

8

Waiting for Mitchell Dunn after school is nauseatingly exciting. Partly because we're waiting for him at the merry-go-round and Jane is pushing so furiously, I think I'm going to barf.

"Stop, stop, STOP!"

"Oh!" says Jane. "You aren't having any fun?"

"NO. Can't you tell?" I throw my head back and drag my heels in the dirt.

"Thrills, thrills. What is it with you girls?"

As we spin to a stop, I catch sight of Mitchell Dunn—once, twice. He's standing with his hands in his pockets, squinting into the sun.

"Why am I here?" he asks.

Even though Jane is the one who asked him to meet us after school, he's talking to me. "We need to ask you something," I say.

He nods. "Yeah, what?"

"You remember when I saw you at the park?" I say.

He lets out a hard, sharp sigh. "What do you think? Jesus. My lip."

"Oh yeah."

"What we want to know is," says Jane, "what's the stuff you heard about Mary Margaret? Didn't you say you heard something?"

He looks at Jane, at me, and back. And then he smacks his cheek. "Why me? Isn't there some girl you can ask?"

"The girls aren't talking to us," I say. "We don't know what's going on."

"So if you know something, be a good guy," says Jane.

Mitchell looks up at the sky, then at Jane. "Okay," he says, expressionless. "They're saying you guys took all your clothes off."

"Who's saying that?" I ask.

"I heard that Shea said you all got into bed together," he says flatly. "And other stuff."

I immediately picture Jane and me and John and Tommy squirming around in bed naked. And then I picture that whole gang of junior and senior boys picturing it . . . and other stuff. Mitchell too. I sit down on the merry-go-round and drop my head into my hands. I'm having trouble breathing.

"You realize that none of this is true, don't you?" says Jane.

Mitchell shrugs. "Just telling you what I heard."

"From Shea?" asks Jane.

"No. From Jerry Conrad."

I moan. Jerry Conrad is an ass. "I hate boys," I say. And when I do, something passes over Mitchell's face. But he then quickly hardens up.

"Just boys?" He squints. "Actually, I hate *everybody*."

Jane turns to me. "The boy is harsh," she says, as if Mitchell's not standing right there.

"Gotta go," Mitchell says. I watch him walk off, loping with those uneven, impatient strides. He's lean, tall, and lanky, and his corduroy pants are just a little too big. And I feel like one of those girls in old movies who stand there with their heart in their throat as the train pulls away.

"Well, now we know," says Jane. "We're being slammed for not putting out."

"Big, stupid Shea." I wrap my arms around my ribs. "Tomorrow I'm going to wear three sweaters, a rosary, and my dad's army jacket."

"No, you won't," says Jane.

"What a dick Conrad is. What a dope."

"Yes, he's a moron," says Jane. "And that's exactly why he's so valuable."

Jane spends our walk home explaining her theory to me. About how Jerry is perfect because he's such a blabbermouth. "He's so gossipy, he's practically a girl. Won't he spread just about anything?"

"I think it depends on what you want him to blab," I say. "We can't go straight to Jerry and tell him we're innocent. He won't care."

"You're right," Jane says. "If he's going to trade in Shea's story about us, he's going to want something just as juicy."

"So what would that be?" I have nothing juicy to trade. Ever. Which is half the problem of my life, I think.

"It has to be something kind of *twisted*. Something so off-the-wall that he'll want to repeat it."

"Ooh. I know. Maybe we can tell him how shocked we were to learn that Shea was born without male reproductive parts. Like a Ken doll!"

"Now we're getting somewhere," says Jane. "Buckle up, Mary Margaret. This is going to be fun."

The next day, we wait outside Sister Eileen's trigonometry class for Jerry Conrad. My first instinct when I see his face is to reach up and break his big black glasses. But instead, I let Jane do the talking.

"Hey there, Conrad," she says slyly.

Jerry immediately flushes and looks over both his shoulders. He obviously cannot believe that Jane is talking to him. "Hey," he says. He brings his books up close to his chest and hugs them nervously, then looks down and drops the books back by his side—for a more manly look.

"You have a few minutes?" Jane asks.

"Uhhh . . . ," he says.

"Oh, come on." She nudges his arm. "It's lunch. Just walk over with us to the church."

"Yeah, okay," he says. He walks with us, stealing sideways glances. If I had to guess what was on his mind, I'd say he was looking at us thinking, *Golly! Girls who get naked are talkin' to me!*

Jane reaches into her bag. "Sucker?" she asks. I try not to smile.

"Sure," says Jerry.

Jane untwists the wrapper and pulls it off. "Open," she singsongs, just like a nurse.

Jerry opens his mouth. Jane slides the sucker over his tongue. He closes his eyes. I think he might pass out.

"Cherry?" Jane asks, unwrapping another sucker for herself. Jerry nods, and the cardboard stick in his mouth bobs up and down. "Mmm. Me too. How about you, Mary Margaret?"

"Uh, no thanks," I say. "So Jerry, you're good friends with Shea, right?" I say, maybe a little too quickly. I gauge Jane's reaction.

"Of course he is," Jane answers. "Everybody knows that." She smiles at him and lowers her voice. "This is why we came to you. We have some stuff we want to talk about. But first, we have to know that you can keep a secret. . . ."

His eyes widen and he blinks quickly. "Sure," he slurs, the sucker still in his mouth.

"Well, you know, last week we had John and Tommy over swimming? And something weird happened. I mean, it was *bizarre*." She puts her hand on Jerry's arm and squeezes. "Promise not to tell?"

Will Conrad swallow his candy, stick and all? "Uh-huh," he says.

"I have these . . . Barbies," she says. "You know, Barbie dolls?"

"Yeah," he says slowly.

"And anyway, I've kept them in my bedroom for a long time—you know, just stuff I used to play with when I was a little girl. So, Mary Margaret and I went into my bathroom to change into our bathing suits, and when we came out . . ." Here Jane points to me. "Oh God. You tell him."

"John Shea plays with dolls," I announce.

"What?" says Jerry, thoroughly confused.

"Yeah," says Jane. "I mean he really, really seems to love dolls, if you know what I mean. If it sounds weird to you, imagine what we thought! We just sat there, watching him comb doll hair. And then he had to have her try on every single outfit in her case. . . ."

"Jane has a million doll clothes," I say.

"He was in there for hours!" says Jane. "We finally just gave up and went swimming with Tommy. We almost asked Tommy about it, but we figured it would be kind of embarrassing for him, having a brother do that."

"Well, that's, uh, not what I heard . . . ," says Jerry.

"Oh really?" Jane asks.

"I heard," he says, taking a gulp, "you all went skinny-dipping. And drinking. And then . . . well, do your parents have a big, round bed?"

Jane drops her jaw. "John said we went to bed?"

"The only one NAKED," I say, using a word that I'm sure will push Jerry over the edge, "was Barbie."

"Honest," says Jane. "Gee, I didn't get the impression he was into real, live girls at all."

"Wow," says Jerry. He pauses, narrows his eyes, and pulls the sucker from his mouth. "Why are you telling me this?"

"She has a big crush on Shea," I say, thinking I sound like a bad actress.

Jane covers her face. "And I just don't know what to think. You know?"

"Oh," says Jerry. "Huh." He shakes his head. "I always thought he was pretty normal."

"So did *we*!" says Jane.

"We thought you might know something," I say. Then I try for a little drama. "I keep telling Jane just to please forget about him!"

"I don't know what to tell you," says Jerry. "Honest."

"Well, that's okay," says Jane. "Just as long as you don't tell anybody else. I *mean* it."

"Oh, I won't," he says.

By the end of school, everybody knows. We're practically celebrities as we walk home. All sorts of people come up to us wanting to hear the story. "No one was supposed to know!" Jane keeps on protesting before repeatedly spilling the beans.

I start to lose my taste for the gag when Connie and Kathy come up to us like we weren't persona non grata just hours ago. They must have reinstated our "worthiness." If boys tell these lies to keep us in our places, then why do girls back them up? It's something I swear I'll never, ever do to another woman.

To make things even creepier, I catch Elizabeth eyeing us as Jane rattles on.

"Jane, I'm gonna go," I say.

Pretending I don't see Elizabeth standing at the gate is impossible. I give her a little stretch-mouthed smile that's supposed to let her know I sort of see her and expect her to blindly step aside as usual. This time, she blocks my way.

"So, which one is it?" she asks.

"Are you actually talking to me?"

"Yes. Is John Shea a homo? Or did you guys have an orgy? Which?"

She's trying to not look squirmy and embarrassed. "Elizabeth!" I say. "*What* just came out of your mouth?"

"*Homo,*" she says, all pinched up. "*Orgy.*" She breathes deep, still fluttery. "See? I can say them."

"Look," I say, "John Shea is not a . . . *homo.* And you really believe that about me? Don't ask me why, but I expected more from you."

"Um"—she blinks—"that's what some boys are saying." Elizabeth waits awhile, all open-minded-seeming, then purses her lips and launches in. "How does she do it? How does she get you to do all these terrible things? How can you stand being talked about like that?"

She is still the exact same little kid who had recurring nightmares about coming to school in her underpants. I feel my heart condense into a piece of charcoal. "So do you believe the dirty gossip?"

"First you have to tell me what happened," she insists.

"All right, Elizabeth. If you really want some news, I do have some for you. None other than John Shea says that you're built like a brick shit house."

Her expression flattens, and I'm glad. Elizabeth hikes up her books like a shield over her enormous breasts. Armored, she shoots me a righteous glance. "What does that mean?"

I shrug. "Just something he said."

Elizabeth seems stuck for something to say. Then I realize she's choking up.

"You're horrible," she says with complete conviction. "I can't believe I was actually worried about you."

"Worried? That's not how it looked to me." I hate that I can't get angry at Elizabeth without her guilting me. I cross my arms and give her the death stare. She marches away. Toward what, I don't know. Righteousness? Salvation?

That evening at home, I'm setting the table and thinking about the fact that if everyone's talking about an orgy and Mitchell's heard it—then he's pictured it, you know? Did he see me as this out-there naked girl, bouncing sexily on the diving board to Wilson Pickett? Or did he see me as the Jane follower, a dope who just got tricked into whatever it was the boys wanted to do? And I realize: I hope he saw me as the diving board girl. Actually hope.

Then Paula comes to the table with a big wet jelly jar full of roses, juicy with perfume. They're Double Delights, from my secret garden. "Oh, Paula," I say. "No."

"What's wrong? They're blooming there all alone on the side of the house," she says, leaning over them for a sniff. "I thought that was a waste."

Of course, she hasn't taken anything that truly belonged to me. There's not an inch of private space on this entire property. But all I wanted was that little patch of dirt. Those roses seemed all the more magical simply because they were my discovery.

"Are you mad at me?" she asks, looking down into the bouquet. "I thought you'd like these."

"They're beautiful, Paula," I say. She smiles and curtsies, then places them in the center of the dinette. I go on setting the table, but the fragrance keeps putting clouds in my head. I sit down and pull the jar toward me. These flowers are more than beautiful. The roses are yellow with deep, red-edged petals. It's as if they're on fire, and all my feelings bloom into a weird, terrible craving.

I stick my face in the middle of the bouquet and breathe in. These are *my* roses. I realize I'm happy. I soak in the rosy perfume and fresh water and grassy leaves. I do that over and over until it's not enough anymore to inhale the smell.

I close my eyes and let the tip of my tongue find the petals. I catch one between my teeth and pull it out. I crush it in my mouth. The texture of the petal feels as tender as skin. I close my eyes again and lower my mouth.

"*What* in the name of . . . ," says my mother.

I look up. Mother stands paralyzed, clutching a dish towel. I can feel a petal poking out of my mouth.

Caught, burning with embarrassment, I spit it into my hand.

"Good God, Mary Margaret," she says in that drop-dead voice of hers. "You don't have to *act it out* for us all." She turns and heads for the living room.

Now I'm not embarrassed. Now I want to kill her.

Mother is surprised when I tap her on the shoulder. She stops picking crayons up off the floor. "Yes?" she says, as if she can't remember us making an appointment.

"So what is it you think I'm acting out?"

"Girls your age are prone to drama." She puts the back of her hand to her forehead. "My feelings!" she says breathily.

My own hand trembles by my side. If she were Kevin or Paula, I'd yank her arm.

"Believe me," I say, "I wasn't putting on a show for *you*. I can't do *anything* around here without a stupid audience."

"You think this is news to me? You'll really see what I mean," she continues, "when you're thirty with five kids. Being alone with your feelings is going to be an impossible luxury."

"You don't get it, Mother. When I'm thirty," I say, with dead certainty, "I'm not going to have any kids."

"Oh really?" she says with a laugh. "What other big plans do you have?"

"Do not *laugh* at me!"

"Foreign correspondent?" She folds her arms. "Botanist?"

I fold my arms in imitation. "Aging, hateful, bitter *drudge?*"

Mother sucks in her breath. I wonder if she is going to slap me.

"It doesn't matter," I say. "I don't care who I turn out to be as long as . . ." I pause. "As long as I'm not *you*."

As soon as I've hit my target, my emotions peak. For the first time in my life, I look at my mother and feel that I'm the strong one. Seeing her now, quiet and slump-shouldered, I feel no shame, no mercy, no sense of victory. "Winning" feels weirdly like nausea.

"I suggest you remember who you're talking to," she says weakly, like she's ready to cry.

Believe me, I say to myself, *I know.*

The next day at school, I feel positively squirrelly. Has this been the longest school year ever? Why did they paint every room in this school puke green? What if it all ended today? I'll take a mushroom cloud. Anything.

"Wouldn't it be cool if this entire school erupted in a fiery conflagration?" I ask Jane.

"Confla-what? Mary Margaret," says Jane, "you're scaring me."

"Or if we could pick up Sacred Heart Academy like a dollhouse—with all the people in it—and drop it into the Columbia River?"

"Oh my," says Jane. She loosens the ring from her finger; it's one she loves, bought from a gum machine, with the face of a grinning rodent molded from orange plastic surrounded by the big, bold words RAT FINK. She slips the ring on my finger and says, "Darling, let me take you away from all this."

"I need to get out of here. I need an adventure."

"And I'm gonna get us one," she says.

Just twenty-four hours later, Jane, all shiny and breathless, catches up with me and hooks her arm in mine. "Practice saying YES," she says.

"Why?"

"I want you to say YES now, without thinking!"

"Yes," I say, closing my eyes. "YES YES YES."

"We're going to a party, Mary Margaret! It's downtown and it'll be full of college guys."

I can feel the smile on my face turning into something else. Jane might as well have suggested parachuting from Crown Point.

"Don't be scared," says Jane.

"I don't think—"

"DO NOT be scared." She clutches me by the shoulders and I am wincing at the strength of her grip. "Please?" she whispers.

I say it. "Yes."

My friend, my best friend, glows back at me. *Oh man, college guys.*

9

Jane already has everything planned. I'll stay overnight with her. Her parents will be out late. We will take a bus downtown to the party—which she learned about from Nancy, a friend from her old school she bumped into at Lloyd Center.

"Rob is Nancy's brother," Jane says. "I'm sure it's going to be a fun party, because he's a fun guy. Tell you the truth, I always liked him so much better than Nancy."

"What's wrong with Nancy?" I ask.

"She's a fair-weather friend," says Jane. "She was supposed to be my alibi when I went off with Roger. But she caved."

"How's that? You got caught in the act," I remind her. "What was she supposed to do?"

"She could have made something up when my mom called. Like say a bunch of us were meeting to drive around all night. Just something to throw everyone off our trail. You would've done it for me."

Would I? I consider. Yes, I'd probably do anything Jane asked.

"Roger and I just wanted to check out everything going on in San Francisco. We planned on coming back. Eventually."

"So," I ask, "was that the end of you and Nancy?"

"Well, she never was actually a great friend. Not like you. It's like all the good stuff went to Rob." Jane stops and shakes her head. "No, I take that back. She's probably smart, but she isn't brave or cool enough to make it *matter*. Like most girls. You know what I mean?"

Like I used to be, I'm thinking.

When it's time to leave for Jane's that Saturday afternoon, my hair is in pigtails, and I'm wearing a pair of Kevin's old jeans. I'm letting Jane make me over when I get to her house. This way Mother won't get suspicious about our plans for the evening.

Jane, however, answers the door wearing one of the most elaborate hairdos-in-training that I've ever seen. Her head's crowded with curlers made from orange juice cans. She has pink tape across her bangs and funny silver clips holding spit curls by her ears.

"Your head looks like a homemade aerospace project," I say.

"Yes, you laugh now, but wait until I comb this out. Truly, I will look just like Julie Christie!" She looks me up and down. "And what's your look?"

"I am your hick cousin Tammy from the cottonwoods," I say.

"All that's missing is the rope belt," says Jane. She beckons me with her finger. "Follow me."

We leave a little trail of footprints across the freshly vacuumed carpet. Every room we pass is in museum-like order and has its own special smell. A mirrored tray of perfumes gives Jane's parents' room a scent that's grown-up and foreign. The bathroom's always Lysol-fresh. Picture frames in the hall give off the oily-clean fragrance of furniture polish. And Jane's room smells like a fabulous store full of brand-new clothes. My house, I suppose, always smells kind of diapery.

In her room, I hear gunfire. Jane's television shows a newscast of rifle-toting boys in helmets crawling on their bellies through a ditch. She takes her remote control and clicks.

"So damn depressing," she says. "I *was* watching *Bandstand*."

"Elizabeth's brother is in Vietnam," I say. "Every time someone's shooting on the news, I look for him." Suddenly I feel guilty, listening to the chatty tone of my own voice. "David is very cool. I bet you'd like him."

"Really? The nun's brother?" says Jane with a shudder. She opens the white louvered doors of her double closet. "What do you want to wear?" I see that the dresses hang together, the blouses and pants and jackets are grouped in their separate niches, and all the hangers face the same direction.

"Can't you imagine that, though?" I persist. "What it's like for his parents, watching news like that every night. You'd never know if you were going to see someone blown up or—"

Jane bares her teeth quickly, a cross between a threat and a smile. "Look, let's think party for now, okay?"

"Whoa," I say.

"I mean, God! I just don't see the point of dwelling on something we can't do a damn thing about." She sweetens. "And I just want everything to be perfect. Just for tonight. Including us." She takes a step back and eyes me, mutely asking for my consent. I nod. Then she pulls something from her closet, something purple.

"Cool color," I say.

"You can try it on," says Jane. "But first . . ."

She does all sorts of stuff to me—and won't let me look! I'm especially spooked when she has me lean over the ironing board to straighten my hair. Because I blink furiously whenever she touches my eyelids, Jane must start over with mascara three times. Big triangle screw-on earrings whang my cheeks each time I turn my head. Finally, I slip on the purple outfit. The pants are bell-bottoms, cut low with a chain belt swinging from the hip. The knit shirt is a paler purple, tight, with psychedelic swirls on the collar and cuffs.

When she turns me toward the mirror, I'm prepared to feel completely mortified. "My God," I say. Here I am, cool and beautiful and practically flawless. My little-boy hips are actually sexy in these low-slung things. I look like someone James Bond would fall in love with. It's a miracle.

"I love it," I say. "I look twenty-two."

"The guys, the *right* guys, are gonna fall all over you. You ARE the ticket," Jane says. "Now it's my turn. And if you so much as touch that makeup, I'll kill you."

Actually, I can't take my eyes off myself. I hold my hand like a gun, scramble to the corner of the floor-to-ceiling mirror, turn and fire, make a sullen kissy face, and whisper, "Hold it right there, Mr. Bond." Who knows? Maybe I can get a job as a ruthless beauty. I don't even hear Jane when she comes up behind me.

"Ciggy?"

I startle. Jane is part Marianne Faithfull, part medieval princess. Her shining hair is half up, half down. And the outfit—a shocking pink Empire-waisted minidress, black lace stockings, gillie shoes with crisscrossed leather laces—is finished with a full-length black velvet cape so long it practically drags behind her like a train.

"You are incredible, Jane Stephens," I say.

She's so happy, full of her own accomplishment. She hands me a Kool and leads me to her parents' mirrored bar. "Vodka and Tab?" she says, holding up a bottle of some Russian stuff. She squints. "Shit. Avery's marked the bottle. Look."

Sure enough, there's a light pencil line on the red-and-gold label.

"I'd just refill it with water if I hadn't done it, like, five times already."

"How much do you drink, anyway?" I ask.

"Every now and then when I'm alone. No biggie. Just enough to make the music sound better."

She pulls out Southern Comfort, Jack Daniels—all are marked with pencil. Finally she locates an ancient, dusty bottle that's half empty and unmarked. "Sloe gin," she says, uncapping it.

I take a whiff. "Ugh." It's like berry cough syrup gone bad.

"What doesn't kill us makes us stronger. And braver," Jane says, filling two old-fashioned glasses with a little Tab and a lot of purple stuff. "Plug your nose and gulp," she says.

She pinches her nostrils and chugs. I do the same. We slam down the glasses at the same time.

"Bring on the boys!" says Jane, twirling in her black velvet.

I'm still gagging. "Wait'll they get a load of us on the bus," I say.

10

Jt's an adventure just walking down the street. Jane strides with her chin up, imperious, breaking character to give me a sidelong glance whenever a car slows down. "This is my mother's," she says, flapping a corner of her cape like a bat's wing. "It's for the *opera*, which I believe she has attended only once."

"Don't you think we look like we escaped from a cartoon or maybe another dimension?" I ask. "In a good way, of course."

"As I see it," Jane explains as we seat ourselves on the bus-stop bench, "we are the real people, in living color. And everybody else? All these boring people going back and forth to the Fred Meyer shopping center? They're strictly *black and white*."

"I just hope my parents don't drive by." Would they even recognize me?

When the bus pulls up, the few old folks aboard don't

even bother to look up as we clunk our change into the glass box.

"Okay, let's pretend," says Jane. "This bus is our Alfa Romeo. Sure, it's big. But it's sporty!"

"And red," I say. "But who are all these people?"

"Our humble servants," whispers Jane. "And we run them ragged. Just look at how *tired* they all are." She puts her thumb to her nose and waggles her fingers at all of them. "So hard to get good help," she says.

The bus is so quiet, it forces you to stare out the window and keep your thoughts to yourself. Now and then, Jane pokes me on the shoulder and wakes me up just to widen her eyes and give me a smile wired with anticipation. We are on the verge of doing something dangerously important. It's as if even the moon knows it and shines on us through the window with a golden awe.

We cross the bridge over the Willamette River, glinting gray as the downtown lights begin to sparkle. "We're getting close, I think," Jane says. We roll through the almost empty business district into Old Town, where, suddenly, the streets seem to host a convention of drunks. Some stagger out of bars, some sleep in doorways.

"This is our stop," Jane says.

"No. Here?"

Jane rings the bell, and the bus lurches to a halt. Before I know it, the doors shut behind us, and we're standing in a wheeze of warm exhaust as the bus rumbles away from us into the dusk.

"We'll walk fast," Jane says matter-of-factly.

To me, our footsteps on the sidewalk seem extraordinarily loud. I try to run on tiptoe until Jane stops me. "Just walk with me," she says. "Try not to look so terrified."

Hail Mary, full of grace. . . . I chant the prayer over and over in my head, hoping all the rosaries I've ever said have worn a shortcut trail to heaven.

"Wait a second," says Jane. "I'm trying to remember if we turn here by the park." She presses her palms to her temples. "Or is it a block down?"

I squeeze my eyes shut as she rifles her memory. Just as I begin to calm to the silence—

"AUUUURRRRGH!" A body sits bolt upright on the park bench behind us! I scream. All I can see is a madman's head, eyes rolling and teeth bared. His hair stands on end, electrified. Like a dog, he forces a vicious growl from deep down in his belly.

"RUN!" shouts Jane. Our feet beat the pavement, and I begin to pick up the thud of an electric bass vibrating on the air. My heart lifts as I race toward the sound.

"UP AHEAD!" yells Jane. "KEEP GOING!"

The music is coming from a little stand of spindly old Victorians with sagging porches crowded between some decrepit apartment buildings. The house in the center is painted in an intense rainbow of colors, and the shutters and door are decorated with smiling stars and suns. It's a gingerbread house in the middle of a dark forest, with great music spilling out of every opening.

"This is it!" Jane leaps in front of me and scrambles up the stairs. She beats on the door with both fists until someone opens the door. "Robby!" she says. She throws her arms around him. He holds her back to take a look.

"Jane?" I notice he doesn't quite look like he was expecting her. His long hair is uncombed. He's cute and has no shoes. The music is loud, and I can hear people talking and laughing inside the house.

"We came for the party," Jane says.

Rob holds a hand to his ear.

"WE CAME FOR THE PARTY!" she screams.

Rob steps out on the porch and closes the door behind him, which barely puts a damper on the noise. "Nancy told me about it," Jane explains.

Rob smiles. "Nancy? That's funny."

"Why?" Jane asks.

"Because she isn't here. I mean, she's never here, hardly. Too many people in and out for her."

"So, this isn't a party?"

"Well, yeah. I guess." He laughs. "It's always like this here on a Saturday night."

"Really? How very cool." Jane giggles, looks over her shoulder at me, and grins. Rob looks down at me with concern, and I immediately know I look like a lost puppy.

"Who are you?" he asks.

"She's Mary Margaret," says Jane. "My best friend."

"Well, come on in, Mary-Margaret-Jane's-best-friend. Come in!" He opens the door, and I feel the drumbeat in my chest. It's "Fire," by Jimi Hendrix. I've heard the song, but I never dreamed how it would sound this *loud*.

71

I have only one burning DESIRE,
Let me stand next to your FIRE.

"Is someone flicking the lights off and on?" I shout.

"Strobe light," Rob explains.

Everyone looks like they're moving through an old home movie. The room's crammed with guttered, dripping candles. Doorways are hung with strings of beads. In the center is an old fireplace, elaborately carved and painted again in those acid rainbow colors; a huge vase of peacock feathers and paper flowers overshadows the mantel. One entire wall displays a giant poster—little pigtailed girls with guns—for the Chinese Communist Party. The other walls have pictures of bands I've never heard of and daisy stickers and all sorts of graffiti. The rug—a big, old, jewel-toned thing with graying fringe—might have been beautiful once. And everywhere, some seated on giant pillows, some dancing alone and some in pairs, some crowded in circles talking close because of the noise, are scraggly kids, almost all of them smoking something and almost none of them wearing shoes. It's the most wondrous place I've ever been.

But man, it smells funny, I say to myself. Not bad, just unfamiliar funny.

I sense that Jane must know how out of place we look, but she seems determined not to fumble or lose step. Thinking we're being laughed at, I go with my first instinct, which is to back up against a wall and attempt to blend in with it.

"Hang here if you want, but I'm jumping," Jane says. "Okay?" She walks up to the most gorgeous guy in the room.

The gorgeous guy is busy talking to a group of mostly girls. He has a mustache, wears a battered brown corduroy jacket, and doesn't bother to brush away the chestnut lock of hair that falls directly over his eye. He seems maybe taller than he actually is and is obviously comfortable with being the center of attention. When Jane taps his shoulder and asks him to light her cigarette, he looks amused and gives her this half smile and says, "Okay, I'll play."

He does light her cigarette, and I can't help but think he's making a big show of his patience. When at last he turns from her to resume his conversation, Jane slips in beside Gorgeous Guy's elbow. Already she's got herself in the middle of something and dumped me.

I'm simmering mad and hating myself for my own wimpiness when, suddenly, five boys park themselves at my feet. I stand for some minutes in the middle of their little cross-legged group, staring like a sphinx into the distance.

"Where's the bathroom?" I finally squeak.

The boys stare up. Not one of them answers me directly. Instead, the guy closest to me takes out this crescent-shaped leather bag, squirts something in his mouth, and hands the bag up to me. "Hey," he says.

I hold the bag at arm's length, trying to figure out what it is. "Hey," I reply.

"Fruit of the vine," he says, grinning slowly like the Cheshire cat.

I'm afraid of staining Jane's shirt, so, squeezing gently, just enough to make the thing drip, I quickly swallow the few sweetish drops that fall on my tongue. It isn't bad stuff; much tastier than sloe gin and Tab. I hand it back to the boy at my feet.

"Hey, little sister, why don't you sit down?" he asks.

I unlock my knees, slide down the wall, and fall hard on my butt. The Cheshire Cat still gives me a blissed smile of satisfaction. In fact, every guy in the group smiles at me that way.

"I'm Gordon," says the cat.

"Mary Margaret," I say.

"I like you, Mary Margaret," Gordon says.

I look from face to face, and it's clear that all these guys have already decided to like me. "Thank you," I say.

"You're welcome," he says simply. And then he hugs me!

"Van," says a chubby-cheeked guy in black glasses. He holds out his warm hand to grasp mine, and soon I'm also being introduced to and hugged by Steven, Wayne, and Neil.

"So, Mary Margaret, you go to school?" asks Gordon.

"Yep," I say, deciding not to say which school. "Do you?"

Gordon chuckles. "Occasionally," he says. "Van and Steven are my roommates, and Wayne and Neil here . . ."

"Just passin' through," says Neil, shaking the hair from his eyes. He's so blond and slim, he's almost see-through.

"From B.C.," drawls Wayne. "Trying to make our way to San Francisco."

"They're crashing at our place tonight," says Gordon. "They're beautiful people."

"How did you guys meet?" I ask.

"How does anyone meet, really?" Neil asks soulfully. "The universe threw us together."

74

"Yeah," says Wayne. "We've been tossed."

"Just like now," says Gordon. "Who knew fifteen minutes ago that I'd be sitting here with a lovely green-eyed lady? Now you're in the circle with me. See how it works?" Gordon spies someone behind me. "Lindy!" he says.

Lindy is wearing a beaded headband and leather bracelets on each wrist. She's carrying a tin pan. "I've been baking!" she says.

Gordon reaches up and takes a brownie. "Thank you, Mrs. Cleaver," he says.

Then Lindy holds the pan out to me.

"Take one," Gordon says. "Lindy makes the best brownies."

"Like, ever," says Van. He chews and smiles, showing brown gooey teeth.

I help myself. When I start to chew, though, I can't believe that Lindy is famous for her brownies. They taste, I don't know, like she got the flour confused with fertilizer.

"Good?" asks Gordon.

"Uh, pretty good," I say.

To wash away the taste, I begin to drink more deeply each time the bag comes my way. And I'm more happy with every passing round. Gordon's so interesting. I love listening to him talk. He asks stuff like, "Hey, Mary Margaret, do you think we knew each other before in another lifetime?" I tell him yes because it feels that way. Sometimes he closes one eye and pokes his forehead, like the way my dad sometimes whacks the side of our old TV to fix the picture. Soon, every time he opens his mouth, I'm laughing.

"Far out," he says whenever I start to giggle.

Van claims to have psychic powers and to have never lost a game of Rock, Paper, Scissors in his life. Wayne, the doubter, tests him and loses five times in a row.

"Are you moving your fingers faster than my eyes can see or what?"

"It's a trick, man," says Neil.

"Or a miracle," I say.

"Maybe it's something I do with my MIND," says Van, his glasses steamed. "With your mere hands, you cannot defeat me."

"The mind," says Gordon, "can be trained, but it cannot be tamed." He lights a homemade cigarette and inhales. "Right, Mary Margaret?" he growls, spewing smoke.

I slap my forehead, just like Gordon. "THAT'S what I've been smelling!" I say, pointing to the cigarette. "You know what, you guys? When I first came into this house, I thought it had a weird smell. It made me think, *OH, MAN, I just do not feel right here.*"

"That's really animal," says Neil gravely. "It's a form of wisdom."

"Smelling is?" I say. "Hmmm, yeah. I never thought of it that way. But anyhow, now everything is good. Re-mark-a-blee good. And you guys are being so great to me and I feel so happy . . ."

"You're trusting your instincts," Neil says. "That's animal."

"Completely," says Wayne.

"Yes!"

The universe has a spotlight where you can stand and

take in all its rays. I am finally in the middle of the center of the perfect place I've always wanted to be.

Standing up, I stumble and have to grab Gordon's head for support. "Where you going?" he asks. The room is twice as packed as when we came. "Don't go!" he says.

As I use my elbows to wedge my body through the crowd, I feel I'm melting into other people I pass. What a heavenly feeling this is, muscling through and touching all these strangers, squishing through to a hallway where people stand in line for the bathroom. The girl in front of me is wearing a bedspread for a skirt. She turns to me, radiating satisfaction, and opens her hands in front of my face.

"I am transparent," she says.

"So am I!" I say, beaming back.

She takes my hand and twirls me, just like my dad used to do when I was a little girl. I twirl her, too. Finally, we put our hands on each other's shoulders and sway to the music, breaking away only to twirl someone next to us in line. Soon the whole line is twirling. We get dizzy and hold hands—all of us in the hallway spread out like in the game Red Rover and swing our arms back and forth. It's like nothing I've ever done. Without saying a word, how can you just walk into a group of people and start a dance? Everything is possible. What if I tried to walk through a wall?

When it's my turn for the bathroom, I realize how badly I need to go. How many hours have passed? I dab wet toilet paper on my face, pinch my cheeks, and try as best I can to comb my hair with my fingers. I have this blasted, faraway look I've never seen before. When I open the door and find

Jane standing there, I nearly jump. I've almost forgotten all about her.

"Mary Margaret," she says. "Where have you been?"

"I've been right here," I say. "Where have you been?"

"I've been changing my life," she says with sincerity.

"Me too!"

"We don't have to take the bus," Jane says. "Isn't that great? Donnie says he'll drive us home."

Donnie, the gorgeous guy, is behind her. He whispers something in her ear and she closes her eyes. I'm full of tremendous goodwill. Donnie is now our friend, my friend. Gee, I like Donnie. . . .

"Okay, let's go," says Jane.

I follow them like a little duckling out the door.

Donnie's van is orange. I like the cartoon flowers on the curtains. The lines on the road are beautiful in the dark, swelling up one after another in the headlights and disappearing under the car. The world outside seems marshmallow-soft. If I were to hurl my body from that speeding van, I know I would bounce as happily as a Super Ball.

Jane turns on the radio. The Beatles sing, "Michelle, *ma belle*. These are words that go together well. . . ." She smokes, gazes at Donnie's profile, and seems to breathe in and out to the music. Her eyes are glistening, as if the song is breaking her heart. Donnie's eyes are on the road, and I'm here in the backseat, watching my best friend fall in love. And me, the duckling, the third wheel, nobody in love with me the least little bit. I start to feel a little less supercalifragilistic.

When the song ends, Jane turns to me and, surprised, asks, "What's wrong?"

"I think I feel a little sick."

"Uh-oh," says Jane.

"Did you girls eat anything tonight?" Donnie asks, glancing at me in the rearview mirror.

"Yes," I say. "Two brownies."

"Lindy's hashish brownies?" says Donnie.

"Yeah," I say. "Lindy's. I think they went bad."

"Mary Margaret! I had no idea," says Jane.

"Let's stop here," Donnie says, pulling over to the Taco Bell across the street from the golf course. "Just run in and get something, anything. You need it. Can you get your door?"

"Sure," I say. "Come with me."

"In a minute," says Jane.

It's good to get outside. After inhaling the cold night air, I begin to feel happy again and way less nauseated. Food will be good, I decide. Blinded by Taco Bell's fluorescent light, I stumble to the back of a line of kids. The boy in front of me has a brown sweater and coppery red hair and even redder ears, and when I realize his hulky friend is one of the Dunn boys, my heart leaps in my chest. I touch him between the shoulder blades. "Mitchell?"

He jerks around quickly and spits out, "What?" But when he sees it's me, his forehead unwrinkles. He's confused, almost. "Hallinan. Where'd you come from?"

"From a van," I say.

"Oh." He cranes his neck to peek out into the parking

lot. He turns back to me and digs his hands into his pockets. "Well, look at you," he says.

I take a step closer to him, entranced by his burning eyes, which seem to have fourteen different kinds of sparkle. "What?" I say.

"You're . . . uh, purple."

"Don't you like purple?" I almost whisper.

"Next!"

He wheels around. I love the way he turns his hands backward on the counter, the way he leans his weight into it, all the angles of his lanky frame. I envy the Taco Bell girl as Mitchell Dunn confides to her his dislike of tomatoes.

The hem of his brown Shetland sweater is starting to unravel. I reach out, thinking of pulling the loose yarn and unspinning him from his cocoon. Instead, I simply hold the hem between my thumb and forefinger as my body fills with electricity.

Mitchell's hulky brother catches me. I smile at him and withdraw my hand. What does he know, anyway?

As soon as Mitchell's food is in the bag, I ask, "Where you going?"

"To the car."

"Can I come?"

He gives me a double take, lifts one eyebrow, and says, "Come here." We step out of line and he lowers his voice. "Are you tanked?" he asks.

"Would that be a bad thing?" I ask.

He sighs and signals to the hulk. "Meet you outside, bro," he says.

I struggle to keep up with him. Finally I grab his elbow and stop him. "Sorry," he says. "I'll slow down."

I clutch his arm. When we get to his parents' Impala, he sets his bag of tacos on the hood. I slide my hands down until they're holding his. Slowly I touch my forehead against his chin and begin to sing.

"Mitchellllllll, *ma belle*. These are words that go together well, my Mitchelllll. . . ." I turn my face up. He looks terrified. "I will say the only words I know that you'll understand," I sing, and I reach for his face. I kiss him. Is he kissing back? I don't even care. I run my hand over his beautiful head and kiss even harder.

He pulls away. "Hallinan, you're killing me," he says. He looks over his shoulder, and when I draw him toward me a second time, he is definitely kissing me back. I feel one of his arms go around my waist and the other across my shoulders. This is nothing like kissing Tommy Shea. During the entire kiss, I'm conscious that this, so far, is the best moment of my life. I feel a simultaneous thrill and panic knowing that this is IT and that it can't last forever. I don't let go of his lips until he stops me.

"Jesus, Hallinan," he says. He lets out a laugh that is something like a whoop. "When did you get so *bad?*"

"I just think you're darling," I say. "I always have."

He wags his head as if he's trying to shake off a dream. "I'm giving you back," he says firmly.

I hold his hand all the way to the van. He knocks on the driver's window, and Donnie opens the door. Donnie doesn't say anything. He waits for Mitchell to talk first.

"You taking these two home?" Mitchell asks.

"I am," says Donnie.

"Is everything all right in there?"

"We're fine, Mitchell," Jane calls.

Instead of talking over Donnie, who sits there like a not-amused parent, Mitchell walks around to Jane's side of the van. "Will you take care of Hallinan?" he asks. "I mean, *can* you take care of Hallinan?"

"Don't worry," she says. "We're going straight home."

He opens the rear door and helps me in. "You didn't hitchhike with this guy, did you?" he whispers.

"No, we met him at this party. You would have loved it," I slur into Mitchell's ear, glad just to get close to him again. "Don't worry."

The hulk is yelling, "HEY, MITCH!"

"You sure you're okay?"

The van starts up, chugging. I put my finger to his lips. "Goodbye, Mitchell," I say. He shuts the door and we lock eyes through the window for as long as we can. Then I slump in my seat and look out at the stars. Darkness . . .

11

I open my eyes and there's Jane's face hovering over me. It's morning. Has she been watching me sleep? How did I get to bed? I raise my palm to her. "Oh, please," I say. "Back up." My breath smells like ether. I smack my lips. "I think I swallowed a blanket."

"You kissed Mitchell Dunn," says Jane simply.

I did. I did kiss Mitchell Dunn. *Mother of God.*

"You kissed him many, many times," says Jane.

This realization creeps up on me in an awful, goose-pimply way. I rub my temples.

Jane kneels down, rests her elbows on the bed, props her chin in her hands, and resumes staring. "What in the *world* were you thinking?"

"I don't remember," I lie. "What did you see?"

"Hmmm. I think I came in about the time you were pinning Mitchell to the hood of his Impala."

Strangely, my thoughts go to Elizabeth. All those sleepover nights where we shyly obsessed over Mitch's secret charms seem to have occurred in another dimension. Who would've guessed that I would be the one to move in, grab him, kiss him—just like that?

"Now don't panic," Jane says. "You were drunk. You can just go back to school and pretend nothing ever happened. I mean, we have less than three weeks left."

Those words pierce my heart. Only three weeks left with Mitch? "Actually," I say, "what if I don't pretend? What if I really, you know, like him?"

Jane looks at me like, *Are you nuts?*

"Hokay," she says, "want me to demonstrate?" She holds up her hands like puppets. "Hello!" says the left hand in a high squeak. "I'm Mary Margaret and I want to be your girlfriend." "Hey!" says the right hand in a deep, nasal whine. "I'm Mitch. Let me introduce you to your ironing board and your seventeen children. You'll be spending the rest of your lives glued together. . . ."

"Ouch," I say.

"Truth hurts, baby," Jane says.

"But he's my crush since my Elizabeth days. We both were madly in love with him from afar."

"Afar is where he should stay. I will not let you throw yourself away on the gimpy neighborhood boy," Jane declares. "Leave him to Her Assholiness. Please."

"Don't call him *gimpy*. That's low."

"Well, excuse me. I prefer a guy who can run faster than I can."

84

"So," I ask, "were you fast enough to pin Donnie?"

In an instant, Jane's expression drains of all fun. "Mary Margaret, it was . . . different," she says in an awed whisper.

"How different?" I ask, a little worried.

"I tried everything. Everything I could think of. And he was so . . ." She shakes her head. "He wouldn't kiss me. He wouldn't give me a thing."

"Oh. Sorry."

She's quiet for a while. And then she says, "He doesn't think I'm good enough."

"Well, then he stinks," I say. "I hate him."

"No, no, it's not like that," Jane says. "What I mean is, he doesn't think I'm *good*. Not honest, or real, or pure, or something."

I make a face to show I'm not following.

"We were talking, you know," Jane says. "We were talking in this big group. It was a weird conversation. Everyone was going back and forth about love. I can't explain what they were saying, really. Someone said something about love having power. You know, like a gun has power."

I watch her fists curl as she talks and I listen harder because I know she needs me to.

"And you know me," she says. "I was really waiting to talk to Donnie all by myself. So when he went to get a drink, I followed him. That's when he stopped and said, 'What do you need?'" Here Jane looks stricken. "And then something happened. It was the simplest question in the world, you know. He made me feel I had to tell the *truth*."

She pauses on that observation. Her eyes are wet, and her voice gets that funny, high, throaty sound that tells you someone is about to cry. "And when I answered, this just floated out: I said, 'I need to be loved.' "

I peer at her expectantly.

"He said . . . *Love is what you have left when you give away everything you don't need.*"

"But how would you do that?" I usually feel I don't have enough—except for the bad things.

Her hand shakes as she wipes her eyes. "I don't know. But I have to see him again," she says.

"Are you sure?" I ask.

"Positive," Jane says. "He's not like other boys. And I'm not like other girls." She flops backward on the bed and stares at the ceiling. "It's just so perfect."

"Then I'm glad, I guess," I say. "The thing I loved about last night is that I felt like everything was starting from zero. And there wasn't one person there who was anything I expected. So it was like I could be new, too. For so long, I've been feeling fatally locked in."

"Isn't it good, saying yes?" Jane asks.

"Actually, I'm thinking of another thing you said to me. Remember? You said, 'I'm changing my life.' "

"Uh-huh," Jane says.

"Oh, Jane," I say, feeling sudden emotion. "You're changing *my* life, too."

She reaches over and touches my arm. We lock smiles until her bedroom door opens. It's Avery, Jane's stepdad, with

half-glasses riding on his nose. He looks around the room briefly. "Breakfast, Jane," he says. "Better get dressed."

Jane tugs her T-shirt down over her underwear as Avery shuts the door.

"Notice how he doesn't knock?" she says coldly.

"No one ever knocks at my house," I say. "Not even to get into the bathroom."

"It's not the same. I'd still rather live at your house," Jane says, and the stuffed teddy bear she throws at the door makes an unexpectedly big bang.

"Really? Why?"

Jane points at the door. "BECAUSE," she says. "I'll tell you a secret. Sometimes, if I'm here like on Sunday morning and Avery is hanging around, I'll go take a tranquilizer and lock my door and fall back in bed. I'd actually rather knock myself out than bump up against him in close quarters."

"Then you'd really hate my house," I tell her. "There's not a square inch of privacy AND no tranquilizers. It's solid, crowded reality in front of your face twenty-four hours a day."

When I do get back home, the hope I have in my heart crouches in a far corner. I feel a sort of shy, yearning embarrassment. Every time the phone rings—will it be him?

But that call never comes, and so by late Sunday afternoon, the ringing phone starts to make me more certain that I've made a gigantic fool out of myself and that Mitchell Dunn finds my attention goofy and hugely annoying and maybe even repulsive.

By the time I wake up on Monday morning, I'm very, very mad.

"Mary Margaret!" my mother yells from the hallway.

I peek out of my bedroom. "Yeah?" I yell back.

"Dentist. Today. After school!" she says. "Don't be late. And make sure Kevin and Paula come home with you." Daniel, who is sitting on her hip, reaches up and covers her mouth with his hand. *Good for you, Danny.*

I squeeze past my mother into the bathroom and find Kevin and Paula are already in there, brushing their teeth and spitting over each other's shoulders. I stand behind them trying to figure out what to do with my hair, pulling it up from side to side.

"Hey," says Kevin. "Give us some room, why don't you?"

Where is that James Bond beauty of Saturday night? The gorgeous new me! What's stopping me from being her right this minute?

"Come here," I say, dragging Paula by the sleeve. "I need you to help me. With my *hair*."

She gives a little clap. "Can we do it like *Dream Girl of '67*?"

So cute. That's her favorite TV show—a yearlong beauty pageant featuring ratted-haired, spider-eyelashed girls in bikinis. "Even better," I tell her. "We'll turn the kitchen into our very own beauty salon."

I lead her to the kitchen and find the rickety ironing board leaning up against the wall. Paula fetches the iron—an old thing that has been dropped so many times, it's barely held together by gunky black electrical tape.

"Okay, Paula," I tell her. "I'm going to brush out a piece

88

of hair, like this." I put my cheek down to the ironing board and brush a hank of hair as flat as I can. "Then you iron. It's simple."

Kevin wanders in. "What are you doing?"

"Making Mary Margaret beautiful!" says Paula.

"Cripes," he says, edging by to grab a bowl of cereal. "Don't let Mom see."

"Back up, Kevin! You're making me nervous." Paula bites her tongue and squints. The old metal iron is heavy for her skinny little wrists. Shaking, she presses down on the lock of hair.

"Don't let it sit too long," I say.

"Girls are insane," says Kevin, crunching on his Wheaties.

She pulls the iron away and gasps. "It looks good!" she says. We keep going. I turn to the other cheek. "I'm getting good at this, I think," Paula says.

"We gotta do my bangs," I tell her. I bend over and rest my forehead on the board. While Paula brushes out my last piece of unstraightened hair, the iron starts to pop. It sounds like a cross between a percolator and a cap gun. "What's that?"

"Hold still," says Paula.

The iron is so noisy now that I picture it throwing sparks. I'm about to say, *Wait a minute*, but Paula brings the iron down. There's a *pfffffffftt!* and a sickening scorched smell. Paula screams and yanks up the iron. I jerk my head up, feeling a jolt of terrible heat.

"Crap!" says Kevin.

"Oh no!" says Paula. Her lip quivers.

"Paula! Dammit! What have you done?"

Aaaagh! I run to the bathroom, holding my head. I might be on fire. I bust open the bathroom door and scare Katie, who has been sitting peacefully on the toilet. "Oh God," I say. "Oh God . . ." A chunk of my bangs has sizzled to a stinky frizz. And glaring in the middle of my forehead is an angry burning triangle.

Suddenly my mother appears in the doorway, a sniffling Paula at her elbow.

I try to get calm. "I'm sorry, Paula, for yelling," I say. "I just—"

"You *ironed* your *hair?*" Mother hollers. "You had *Paula* iron your HAIR?" She's almost breathing fire herself.

"I need ICE!" I scream.

My mother follows me all the way to the fridge. "*What* in the *world* possessed you to . . . Don't you have an ounce of *common sense?*"

I whack the old metal ice tray against the counter while she nags and complains. I run with the ice to my bedroom and cry.

Paula comes in and puts her hand on my shoulder. "I'm sorry, Mary Margaret. I'm so, so stupid." Her eyes are glittery and her nose is red. "I didn't mean to hurt you."

"Paula," I say, clapping my hand on hers, "you aren't stupid. Don't ever let people make you feel stupid. Especially me."

She nods quickly, wiping away a tear.

Katie, who has been standing in the doorway, brings out her scruffy blue bunny from behind her back.

"Mr. Julius," she says. "He healed my stitches."

Katie places Mr. Julius on my chest. She smiles as I throw my arms around both my sisters and kiss their foreheads. How my mother gave birth to two such nice little girls, I'll never know. I am less of a mystery.

"Look, Katie," says Paula. "Mary Margaret is better! Mr. Julius really works!"

12

J walk to school that morning with a bikini scarf tied around my head, going over how I'll get through this day. The burned hair is chopped short, and the rest is combed down in order to camouflage the dark pink triangle.

"New look?" asks Jane as soon as I catch up with her at the Cyclone fence.

"I ironed my hair," I say. "But I ended up ironing my head."

Jane peeks under my bangs. "Ow."

"Vanity. Apparently one of the deadlier sins."

It is amazing how little you have to see if you refuse to look around. I look at my hands in church, at the board and at my books during finals.

At lunch, I ask Jane, "Is Mitchell Dunn anywhere in the area? Because I want to sit in the opposite corner of wherever he is."

"Don't worry," she says. "He hasn't even looked at us once today."

"Ah. Great," I say, completely relieved and utterly disappointed.

"All we have is a little more than two weeks of school left," she says. "Just think about that."

"Fabulous," I say.

"And Saturdays . . ." Jane sighs. "We'll have whole weeks of them."

She's thinking of that house downtown and Donnie.

"Jane," I say. "What would you have done if Donnie had just ignored you? When you walked up to him at the party."

"I wouldn't allow for that to happen."

"That's ridiculous," I say. "You're not in charge. You know? Of everybody's reactions."

"I'm not saying I'm in charge."

"Yes, you are," I say. "Take me. If I'd gone over to Donnie . . ."

"But you wouldn't have." Jane shrugs. "See? You pick the people you want to know or to love or whatever it is. And you positively erase the doubt from your mind. I don't know how to explain it, except to say"—she outstretches her palm—"if you will it, they fall like ripe fruit." She pauses. "At least that's what the Chinese say. Saw it once on Channel 10."

The Chinese and Channel 10 must know. Because I remember Jane sitting by me in church on her first day of school. There I was, droning away at prayer, robotically sitting, standing, and kneeling on command. Who could have guessed how ripe for a change I was? Jane fastened her large blue eyes on my face, crossed herself, and smiled. "In the

93

name of John, Paul, George, and Ringo," she said. And I fell from the tree directly into her hip pocket.

I drop both fists on the table. Where is that damn Mitchell Dunn?

I scan the crowd until I find the back of his red head and send pounding thought waves. I am thought-waving with all my might.

Oh my God. He turns!

I smile. He reddens. I wave. He nods once, quickly.

Jane does a double take. "What's going on with you?"

"I gotta talk to him," I say, never taking my eyes from his. I toss my head to show him I want to meet him behind the church.

Mitch draws in his chin. "Now?" he mouths.

Yes.

"Well, make it short and sweet," Jane says. "No sobbing, as in the younger Shea." She sends me off with a wave of her hand.

I try breathing normally while I press my back against the church's brick wall. When Mitchell Dunn appears, I thrill to how he straightens his arms and stuffs them deep into his pockets. I love how he leans back on his heels. From the stony way he stares down at me, though, I feel like this may not go well.

"What?" he asks.

I dutifully erase all doubtful thoughts. "Saturday night," I say. "I thought you liked it. I mean me. *It.* You know."

A crease appears between his eyebrows. "Is that a question?"

"Actually, no." I uncross my arms. "It's a statement." My

face is burning as hot as my stupid forehead. "I like you, Mitchell Dunn. A lot."

"You were drunk," he says. "A lot."

"Well, yeah," I say. "But still . . ."

"That friend of yours," he says. "Does she know what you're back here saying?"

"No," I say.

"Because you know, Hallinan, you've changed. Ever since Jane what's-her-face."

"What do you mean?"

"C'mon," he says irritably. "I can tell that now you're the kind of girl who needs to dress up in purple clothes, and have some guy who'll make a big deal about how beautiful you are, and put a lot of time into boyfriend bullshit like dances. Yeah, and picking you up in a suit and giving you a corsage thing in a plastic box. And listening to goddamn KISN and double-dating. All that shit. I'm telling you right now, I don't do that."

"I have no idea what you're talking about," I say.

"I don't *dance!*" he shouts.

I lean toward his face. "So, WHO ASKED YOU TO?" I shout back.

"So . . ." He trails off, puts a finger in his ear, and jiggles it. "Man, you're loud," he says, sort of smiling.

"Never try to outshout a Hallinan," I say.

"That right?" he says. Then, recovering his bad temper, he says, "Like I was saying, I don't dance. Now. Are we through?"

"NO, we're not." I reach down and grab his wrist. "Listen

to me. I don't know who you think I am. But it's okay with me if we never dance. It's okay."

He stands still and listens.

"And another thing," I say. "I don't want any boyfriend bullshit, either. In fact, I don't want a boyfriend. And please, no corsages. If you want to see me, I'd be so happy, but I don't care if we call it a date. In fact, I'd rather not. Everything normal makes me sick, anyway. Truly. God, tell me you know what I mean!"

He shakes his head, incredulous. "Yeah," he says, brightening. "I do."

"No normal," I say. "No commercials for normal. I don't want to be in the movie about normal." I let go of his wrist.

Mitchell cocks his head, then gently claps his hands on my shoulders. "Okay, Hallinan," he says. "I'm still right about *this*, though. You really have changed."

"Yes," I agree. "Like you wouldn't believe. Hey, just wait until I take you to this house—"

But I can't talk because there's this clank against my teeth and I'm looking at Mitchell Dunn's closed eyelids. He's . . . kissing me.

I'm whirling dizzy, barely holding up the church wall when Mitchell walks away. Wow. And this is exactly what I want—coming and going whenever we feel like it. No walking around attached at the hip. *No boyfriend bullshit.* We'll be revolutionaries! Except, I still don't know if I want to tell Jane.

"Was it painful?" Jane asks when I wobble back.

"Not at all," I say.

"You look shell-shocked."

"Do I?"

I could tell Jane what happened, but I don't want to hear a discouraging word. This new feeling is mine, mine, mine, and I just want to pulse with it as long as it lasts.

The rest of the day, it's like my brain swallowed an Alka-Seltzer. Everything's fizzy and sparkly. After school, I keep wrapping my arms around Katie and Paula and riffling their hair on our way to Dr. Fleiner's. Kevin, of course, dodges me.

"Jeez, Mary Margaret," he says. "Have you gone mental?"

I smile. Even the chemical scent of the dentist's office smells like love.

And then we get home.

Katie bursts in the door first, yelling, "No cavities!"

I follow her and notice immediately that there is no TV on. No dinner cooking.

"Mommy!" Katie shouts.

She wakes Daniel, whose fussing we can now hear from my parents' room.

Paula runs down the hall. "Mom isn't here, either," she says.

Now all of us kids are standing shoulder to shoulder around Daniel's crib. "Do you think she might have gone next door?" I ask.

Paula runs to the window, lifts the lace curtain, and taps on the glass. "Mom!" she squeals.

"She out there?" Kevin looks over Paula's shoulder.

"Let me see." I push both of them aside. She's there, all right, sitting on a bunged-up summer lawn chair, staring.

The cigarette she holds between her fingers has a very long ash. "Paula, change Danny," I say. "I'll be right back."

"I'm coming, too," says Katie, tugging my skirt.

"No, Katie. Stay here with Paula. She'll appreciate your help."

Paula catches my firm glance. "Come here, Katie," Paula says as I head outside.

When I open the door to the backyard, Mother finally looks up. Her face, though tear-streaked, is now completely dry. "Mom?" I say. I inch closer, then kneel. "Everything okay?"

"Fine," she says.

"What happened? Is it something with Daddy?"

She tilts her head to her shoulder and gives me an exhausted glare. "DADDY," she says, "is just fine." Suddenly she flings her cigarette and puts her finger in her mouth. "Dammit!" she says, wincing.

"Burned?" I ask.

"BURNED," she confirms loudly, as if I'm an idiot child.

"Sorry," I say.

Mother looks over her shoulder. "Is everybody home?" she asks.

When I say yes, she mutters to herself, "Can't do this, cannot do this."

Now I watch Mother reach down for her purse. "I'm going on errands. Tell your father," she says.

When I come back inside, Kevin asks, "Where'd Mom go?"

"Errands," I say, as if this were a normal thing. "She said she wants everyone to do their homework right now."

"But I'm hungry," he whines.

"Get Paula and Katie, sit down, and I'll make you something."

Paula puts Daniel in the high chair; I make cinnamon toast. Katie sits with her tongue sticking out, doing her math. My goal is to keep them all busy and not asking questions. Everything's quiet and uncrazy—but creepily so.

Kevin cracks open his social studies book and scratches his head. "So, where did you say Mom was?"

"Car repair," I say.

"Oh," says Kevin, satisfied.

I'm so glad to hear Dad's car in the driveway.

"Hello, kid-diddles!" he says, sweeping Katie up. Paula hugs him around the waist. "How's my Hallinannies?" He spots me sponging down the sugary counter. "Say, Mary Margaret. Where's Mom?"

Kevin pipes up. "Car repair."

"What?"

"I dunno," Kevin says. "Something with the station wagon."

"Where's dinner?" Dad asks, looking lost.

"We're on our own," I say.

Dad gets serious. "When did Mom leave?"

"At three-thirty," I tell him.

My father puckers his mouth to one side—his worried face. And then, as if a light goes on behind his eyes, he announces: "Everybody in the truck for A&W!"

"Yaaay!" says Katie. Kevin and Paula bump into each other running to get their coats.

Mom's still not home when I help Dad put the kids to bed. I can't sleep until I hear her come in the door at twelve-thirty in the morning. Though I can't make anything out from her mumbling, I do hear my dad say, "Cynthia! You went out drinking by yourself? At the Flame?"

I wonder if Paula heard that. Mother maybe drinks eggnog at Christmas. Is she drunk? Then her bedroom door slams, and I think Dad rustles around for another half an hour. In the morning, I find him lying on the couch.

He raises his head and puts his finger to his lips. "Shhh," he says. "Let's let Mom sleep. Help me make breakfast?" He gets up and motions me over to the dinette and sets the table.

"I heard Mom come in last night."

Dad pulls out the sugar bowl and puffed rice.

"Dad," I say again. "I heard *everything*."

He shushes me.

"She went to the Flame?" I'm determined to make him talk when Katie and Paula appear, shivering in their night-gowns. Kevin stumbles after them.

"Where's Mommy?" asks Katie, frowning.

"Sit down," whispers Dad. "You too, Kevin."

I remain standing. When everyone else is seated, he sounds official. "Kids," he says, "we have to be extra nice to Mommy nowadays."

"We're *always* nice to Mom," protests Kevin.

"Extra nice, Kevin," says Dad. "Mom's going to be a little more tired. . . ."

Oh my God.

". . . might just need a little more of our help. . . ."

The floor starts to blur.

". . . good news is, you're getting a new baby brother or sister!"

Paula and Katie hold hands and squeal. Kevin wrinkles his nose.

"Where are we going to put it?" he asks.

I say, "Excuse me."

A quick tiptoe up the hall and I'm leaning against my mom's bedroom door, my hand on the knob. I open it a crack and watch her for a few seconds, her black hair unpinned and spread across the pillow. She looks dead. I'm sickened.

If I could help her, I swear I would. She can't want another kid any more than she wanted me. *Why don't you stop?* I want to yell.

She's barely breathing. The room smells stale. I need to leave this place. Right now.

13

"Why," I ask Jane, "doesn't your mom have a ton of babies?"

"First of all," Jane says, "she doesn't want any. She'd rather spend her time polishing Avery's throne."

"I don't think my mother wants any more babies, either," I say. "But she keeps on having them. That's what Catholics do."

"Don't some of them try not to have sex on the days you can have a baby?"

"Then they should just stop having it."

Jane raises her eyebrows.

"My parents are so old, and they hardly even like each other, anyway. I don't see the point."

"Let's see, if you're a normal person, there are always rubbers. That's usually your first choice. And if you have a responsible-type guy who doesn't want to spend his life chained to you, he'll show up with them."

"My dad is already chained."

"Actually, my mother's solution is a good one," Jane says. "Diaphragm."

"What's that?"

"You are kidding. Right?"

I shake my head no, feeling a little stupid.

"It's birth control, sweetie. Like the Pill. You have heard of the Pill, haven't you?"

"Of course. Everyone knows about the Pill," I say. "But it's a sin to take it. Aren't your parents Catholic?"

"Barely," she says.

"But don't they feel bad . . . killing babies?"

"Who's killing babies?" Jane stares at me. "Do you think the Pill *kills* the baby?"

Yes, that's what I think. Doesn't it?

"Oh dear, Mary Margaret."

Jane says this so tragically, it makes me unexpectedly angry. "Don't feel sorry for me, Jane."

"Okay," says Jane in a placating tone.

"Also," I say, gathering my strength, "also—I have a huge passionate thing for Mitchell Dunn!"

"Wha—?" Jane throws her hands in the air. "Now you've lost me."

"I wasn't going to tell you," I say, feeling a blush taking over, "because of what you think about him."

"You're wrong there," says Jane. "I mean, I don't think of him. At all."

"What a snotty thing to say!"

"Mary Margaret, I don't believe you've thought this through. What, exactly, is the *point* of Mitchell Dunn? In one sentence."

I don't hesitate. "I'm crazy about him."

"You know all this from one drunken night at Taco Bell?"

"Um, there's more. We've been getting together." I scrunch up my shoulders. "Secretly."

"You're kidding." Jane, obviously disappointed, tucks a fallen strand of hair behind my ear and gazes at me as if I'm feebleminded. "Don't forget about what we're trying to do here. You and me, we're going to be a new kind of people. With Mitchell Dunn, where are you gonna end up?"

"What you don't get, Jane," I say, "is that Mitch wants to be a new kind of person, too. He told me no boyfriend bullshit and he means it. We're not going to do the Sacred Heart going-steady, get-a-ring, get-married crap. He's different. You'll see."

Jane shakes her head urgently.

"Just give him a chance is all I'm asking. Because I want to take him over to Rob's house this weekend."

"As your date?"

"No. We don't date."

"Do you think he'll even like it there?"

"I really think so," I say. "He's ready for change, I'm telling you. School's almost over, and I want to start the summer off right by showing him that place. And besides, then we won't have to take the bus."

This makes Jane open up a bit. "Well, the no-bus thing is definitely in his favor."

"He has other qualities, too."

Jane eyes me doubtfully.

"You'll see," I say. "You'll see! Even you don't know everything, Jane Stephens."

"*Okay*, Hallinan. For you, only for you."

Regardless of the fact that Mitchell is NOT my boyfriend, my parents show some alarm as his car stops in front of the house.

"See ya," I say, heading out.

"He's not coming to the door?" My mother addresses this question to my dad, who puts on an official father voice.

"Your new friend has got to come to the door, Mary Margaret."

I blow my bangs out of my eyes and stump out to the car. Mitch seems surprised when I ask him to roll down the window. Seeing him there in real life, head to foot, I want to fall upon him and devour him.

"What's up?" he asks.

"Mitchell, I am so sorry. But my parents insist you come to the door."

He closes his eyes. "Oh man."

"It's not my fault." I take his hand and pull him to his feet.

My father is waiting on the threshold. I know he's just putting in pointless "door time" for Mother's sake.

"Sir?" says Mitch. He stands military-straight and holds out his hand. "I'm Mitchell Dunn. Nice to meet you."

Dad smiles, surprised. I'm wondering, Where did *this* Mitch come from?

"Well, I've seen you in church for years, but I didn't put the name and face together. You two will be back by twelve?"

"Yes," I say. "And Jane's coming, too, you know."

Dad just stands there, presumably wondering what he's supposed to ask next.

"We're going to go now, Dad," I tell him.

"Pleasure meeting you, sir," Mitch says. "I'll have her home on time."

"All right. Okay. Sounds good," Dad says. As Mitch turns, Dad gives me the A-OK sign.

Back in the car, I say, "Hmmm. I had no idea you could be so . . . traditional."

"It's nothing. My dad's that way. We grew up saying sir."

No one is required to go to the door for Jane. "Hey there, Mitchell," she says, ducking into the backseat. I'm surprised at her appearance: no opera cape or space-girl hair. Her face is so scrubbed, you can see the freckles across her nose.

Jane gives directions to the bridge, over the river, into the city. Mitch tells us this is his first time driving downtown.

"I'm shocked!" Jane says.

I turn sharply and give her a warning look. "Take a left here, Mitch," I tell him. "The house is in the middle of the block."

Mitch slows to a crawl in front of the electric Rainbow House. On the sagging porch, beneath the painted sun and stars, barefoot kids are sitting outside blowing bubbles and drinking from bottles while the lights inside the house flash bright and dark.

"This house?" Mitch asks.

Jane giggles.

"Yes," I say. "Believe it or not."

"Lucky me," says Jane. "I get to go absolutely anywhere I want as long as I say I'm going with Mary Margaret."

"Her parents think I'm wholesome," I explain.

After we park, Jane jumps out the back and gallops ahead. Mitch sits.

"You ready?" I ask.

He joins me on the sidewalk. With his hair grown as long as his father will allow, his Wrangler cords, and his scuffed Converse sneakers, he might be the most clean-cut kid on this block. I can see him checking out the house one last time. "Let's go," he says. Determined, he limp-marches up the stairs and pushes open the front door.

"It's you!" says Gordon, pointing. Mitch looks over his shoulder.

"He means *me*," I shout over the music.

Gordon's sitting on the floor exactly where I left him. He pats the rug by his thigh. "Welcome back!"

I haul Mitch over. "This is my friend Mitchell," I tell him. Gordon holds out his hand. "Welcome, man!" he says, and offers him the wine bag.

"Nah," says Mitch. "Thanks. But Mary Margaret here, she's the heavy drinker."

Calmly I take the bag and squirt it down my throat like an expert.

"She's working on her alcoholic merit badge, actually," he says.

"He just doesn't want to crash his parents' station wagon," I say.

The girl sitting on the floor behind Gordon taps him on the shoulder and passes him a collapsed cigarette. He smiles like a saint, inhales and holds it in, then passes the cigarette to Mitchell.

"Is this pot?" Mitch asks me.

"Try it," says Gordon. "You can absolutely drive when you're stoned. It's nothing like drinking."

"Are you sure?" I ask.

"Completely safe for operation of a motor vehicle," drawls Gordon.

Mitch hesitates a few seconds, then raises the joint to his lips. The tip glows red, and his eyes water. He exhales with a choke. "Nasty," he says.

I want to try. The smoke burns going down, but I'm a smoker, after all. I don't choke.

"Looks like you've already earned your marijuana merit badge." Gordon cracks himself up.

"Do you want to look around?" I ask Mitch. Gordon insists we take the joint with us. We end up in the crowded, tin-ceilinged kitchen with the chipped tile walls and a four-legged farmer's sink. Crickets chirp in a cage hung from a hook. Jungle plants are growing on an old card table. We plop on a velvet couch with the stuffing hanging out.

"You're getting the hang of smoking, I see." I watch

Mitch's profile in the half-light, see how he lifts his square chin when he takes a drag.

"Full moon," he says, gesturing toward the window. "I've never seen it so big and mmm . . ."

"And cratery," I say decisively, taking the joint for myself.

"It's, like, completely damaged and shot full of holes," he says. "Sort of like this place."

"But still," I say, "the moon is in a good mood. Look at the shine."

"Share?" asks Rob, reaching for the joint. He hugs me, grabs Mitchell's forearm in a brotherly handshake, plops down by him, and the two start talking. About what, I'm not sure. The room's become too loud and my own breathing suddenly fascinates me.

I take Mitch's hand and turn it palm up. In and out I breathe, tracing the deep lines with my finger. If I study it long enough, will this palm reveal the map of the universe?

"Mary Margaret," says Mitch. Rob's gone now, and Mitch locks eyes with me. I feel I've come back from a good, long vacation. Mitch smiles at me, far away and close at the same time.

I cup my hand to his ear. "You should smile more often, Mitchell. It makes you look, I don't know. Angel-like. Anyway, you happy?"

"I think pot makes you think you're happy," says Mitch.

"Uh-huh." I yawn. "But isn't that good enough? I really think my mom should smoke a joint."

"Why?"

"Because she has no inner sunshine. I mean, her blinds are *down*. Now look around at all these pot-smoking people. They've lifted the curtains and opened the windows. It's, like, freeing."

"I see what you mean about the people here," says Mitch. "Like that guy Rob. He's all right. You know, I've met two guys so far, and neither of them asked me if I play basketball."

"That's good?"

"Yeah." He scowls. "I hate it when people ask me that."

"I guess you tall guys get asked that a lot," I say, and I feel Mitch's body go rigid.

"Well, I don't play," he says.

Even though I'm high, I don't have the guts to bring up the polio thing. I wonder if I ever will. You know how you can tell when someone has something that's just off-limits?

I glance at the window. "Look. That moon's just getting bigger. Weird. If you didn't know how there's light shining on it from the sun," I say, "you'd think it's lit from the inside."

Me, I feel lit from the inside.

"Let's go out in the yard and look at it," says Mitchell.

The grass in the backyard is unmowed and spring green. An airplane passing over the moon makes a furnace-warm sound. The air is body temperature, and "Heart Full of Soul" streams through the open doors and windows.

The guitars sound gypsy or Indian. Behind us, ivy has grown over a plum tree and the vines form a little cave. "Come in," I say.

I wait, watching Mitch as he crawls in. He sits close, and

I lean into him. He wraps his arm around me and I think I might die of happiness.

"Have you noticed everyone's always touching you at this place?" he asks.

"You mean all the hugging and shaking hands? I like it."

"We don't do that at my house," Mitch says. "Ever."

"Here, nobody's angry," I say. "It makes me feel like I never want to go home."

Mitchell reaches over and cups my face for a moment. His eyes are blue ice in the dark, but the intensity of his stare is almost too much for me.

"Do you know," I say, "that I can feel your electricity? I've felt it for a long time. When you're in any room I'm in, it buzzes me. It even wakes me up at night sometimes. And right now, it's coming from over here"—I touch his forehead—"and here." I put my hand on his heart.

He lays his hand on my knee. "God, I want to touch you," he says.

Every part of me wants to be touched.

"Start here," I say, holding out my hand. He kisses it.

When Mitch's shirt comes untucked, I put my hand up there. He does the same to me. My skin goes on forever, it seems. I'm thinking that after all these years, I've found out what skin is actually for.

I impulsively lick Mitchell's neck. He pulls back. "Did you just *lick* me, Hallinan?"

"Me? No," I say.

He wipes his neck with the back of his hand. "Yes, you did," he says. "I'm wet."

I press my lips together, trying not to laugh.

"How'd you like it if I slobbered all over you?" he says.

"Let's find out," I say.

He narrows his eyes, then licks me all over my right ear. It sounds and feels like a warm ocean.

"You're a bit of a dribbler yourself," I say, pulling back.

"Come here," he says. Then we're at it again.

"Mary Margaret?" I hear Jane calling my name from somewhere out there. Talking seems to be a vastly inferior way of communicating.

"Over here!" I call as Mitch readjusts his lower jaw. My own face is feeling stingy and scraped.

Jane, holding a slim paperback to her chest, peeks in. "I've been looking for you all over. It's a quarter till twelve."

"Wow. Guess you've been to the library."

"This?" Jane holds out the paperback. There's a kneeling stone statue on the front. *Siddhartha*. "Donnie gave this to me to read."

I scramble out from our den of leaves and brush the grass from my clothes and hair while Mitchell hunts for his lost keys. I take Jane aside. "You got a reading assignment?"

"Mary Margaret, are you making fun of me?" says Jane, serious.

"No. I . . . Never mind. I don't have words."

"You're stoned," says Jane. "Brownies again?"

"No. We were smoking. Me and Mitchell." I lower my voice. "See? I told you he was open."

There's stirring in the ivy cave. "Found 'em," cries Mitch, jangling his key chain. He holds my hand as we walk along.

112

"What did you do with Donnie?" I ask when we're back in the car.

"We spent a lot of time in his room."

"All right!" I say.

She slaps my arm. "But not like that. No."

"Then like what?"

"Well, he told me I was beautiful. . . ."

Mitchell, at the wheel, rolls his eyes as he starts the car.

"That's because you ARE beautiful," I say loyally.

"And then he said that like most beautiful girls, I think I deserve to rule without first learning how to serve."

"Huh?"

"And he also said I don't have any sense of history and . . ." She pauses, racking her brain. "Oh, and that I'm spiritually undeveloped."

"Did you slap him?"

"No!" Jane insists. "He's right."

"Jane, are *you* on drugs?"

"My head is clear. There's nothing I'd rather do than sit and listen to him talk."

"You got to talk, too, right?"

"Yes. Sometimes."

"But he sounds so insulting."

"Everything Donnie says," Jane declares serenely, "he says out of love."

"So, can you girls maybe save this conversation for later?" Mitch is hunched over the steering wheel, blinking. I look at his speedometer. We're going twenty-nine miles per hour on the Markham Bridge—eleven less than the speed

113

limit. The water's a long way down. "I'm gonna need total silence to get us home in one piece," he mutters.

"I just want to go back and see him next week," Jane whispers.

The car behind us honks, shines its brights, and passes.

"Jesus!" says Mitch. "I'm only going thirty miles an hour. Does it *feel* like I'm going thirty miles an hour?"

"Actually, Marijuana Boy, it feels like twenty-five," Jane says.

"Shhh!" I make a face at Jane. She draws her fingers across her lips with a zip.

I start to say Hail Marys, but without my usual bargaining promises. Because deep in my heart, I already know that if I do make it home in one piece, I'm not going to be good.

14

The weather is perfectly blushy and beautiful, and the end of school is so near, I can't concentrate. This sunbeam has penetrated my brain, blinding me to everything but thoughts of Mitchell Dunn.

He's never far away, but we're relating even from afar. He'll look at me and bite his lip. My heart will go *bump bump* and I'll twist my hair. He'll walk by and say, "What's for lunch?" And I'll think, *I want you for lunch*. It's like we're thinking the same stuff, but we aren't letting anyone in on our private thing.

I know I'll never be wearing his ring with a bunch of tape wound around to make it fit. We won't be walking each other to classes, and I won't (ugh) put homemade cookies in his locker. When we get together, it's after school and usually somewhere weird. Like the Texaco station.

Lately I've been walking with Jane almost to her house, then telling her I'm going to the Texaco to get a Pepsi from the machine. Mitchell waits for me there. We smile, then drag each other into the bathroom and make out furiously.

Now, just the lavatory smell of Lysol and powdered soap makes me so turned on, I want to take my top off. Is this normal?

A few days ago, we were taking turns pinning each other against the wall, banging against the door and ferociously kissing. Once, by accident, I pushed the small of his back into the doorknob. He howled.

Next thing we knew there was some mad knocking. It was the Texaco mechanic. I opened the door to say *everything's okay*, but he turned us out onto the pavement, forcing me face to face with Elizabeth's big blue family station wagon.

Elizabeth's dad seemed not to recognize me, but her mother did. Elizabeth sat in the middle seat with her arms folded. Like I feared, her mom buzzed down the electric window and waved. "Hey there, Mary Margaret!" she said cheerily, as if I never stopped coming over after school.

"Hey!" I said, trying to smile like I didn't just step out of a locked gas station restroom, my hair in a nest and my clothes messed up, with a *boy*.

I watched her poke Elizabeth on the shoulder and point to me. Mitch took that exact moment to hold my hand. And then I knew: *Elizabeth's still hung up about Mitch.* She turned away from me slowly, hanging her head. This crushed me. It was almost as if I had reached out and slapped her. Even now, it doesn't make me feel any better realizing she was probably going home to cry. I'd do the same thing.

Should I feel guilty? I ask myself. At least when summer

comes, I can avoid her completely and see Mitch as often as I want.

But as it turns out, getting away from my past proves to be not that easy.

The next morning at school, my homeroom teacher, ancient, no-nonsense Sister Cecilia Alice, makes a beeline to Jane and me after morning mass.

"Stand up straight," says Jane. "Here comes Sister Tequila Elvis."

"Stephens and Hallinan," says Tequila Elvis. "You two are still on altar duty, I think?"

"We are," I say.

"You should know, then, that we're going to need you on Friday after school for rehearsals. We're practicing crowning the Blessed Mother, and we are going to require some extra help with the little girls."

Jane is quick. "This Friday?" she says. "My mother and father and I are going to be visiting my grandparents in Klamath Falls." She turns to me. "We were just talking about it!"

"Oh, dear," Sister says. "I'll have to find someone to take your place, then, Jane."

"I'm so sorry," Jane says.

When Sister takes off, Jane shakes me by the elbow. "Why didn't you say something? Don't tell me you want to babysit after school!"

"I didn't have time to think," I say. But the truth is, the Crowning of the Virgin is a really pretty ceremony. Eighth-grade girls choose first-grade girls as their attendants. There's a procession and song to Mary, Queen of Heaven, as the girls trail up the aisle in their formals. The oldest eighth-grade girl wears white and is the May Queen, who places a crown of flowers on the statue of Mary. I had loved being an attendant.

Some schools have cut out this ceremony because modern Catholics are putting Mary in the background. Father Dreiser, being of the old school, still hangs on to Mary Day. This suits Paula fine. She's always trying on my old dotted Swiss gown and twirling in front of the mirror, dreaming of her own eighth-grade day in May.

In class, the first thing Tequila Elvis does is ask for a Mary Day helper. And the first person to raise her hand?

"I'd be glad to help," says Elizabeth.

"Oh boy!" Jane whispers. "Fun with the nun!"

Then Mitch catches up with me after class to let me know he's found a Texaco replacement. He's got the car Friday after school.

"Damn," I say. "I'm helping with Mary Day rehearsals."

"Can't you get out of it?" he asks.

I tell him there's no way and watch him seethe a little. "Maybe after rehearsals?" he says.

We decide he'll pick me up at church at five-thirty.

On Friday, I run to get to the church vestibule before Elizabeth does, figuring that if I can get busy with something, we can avoid any awkward small talk.

It's obvious the eighth-grade girls are good babysitters already. Some are sitting on benches, holding the first graders in their laps. Others are holding hands with the little girls and introducing them to the big ones. It's like a mother-daughter tea.

A few little girls run around like meteors, chasing each other around the big girls' legs and laughing. Then I see Elizabeth.

In moments, she has one of the girls by the shoulders and is whispering in her ear. Soon Elizabeth is smiling as the whole bunch of first graders gather in front of her. With their eyes wide open and their mouths closed, the girls are clearly in awe of her.

"Okay," Elizabeth says, "we're going to play a game. When you see me touch my nose and raise my other hand like this . . . then you do the same thing. Can we try it?"

The girls all copy Elizabeth's pose. Quite a few are giggling.

"The trick is," Elizabeth says, "to hold your breath and be perfectly quiet as soon as your finger touches your nose. So watch me, okay?"

The girls wait as Elizabeth stands with her hands by her side. As soon as a few girls start to chatter, Elizabeth's right hand shoots up and her left hand touches her nose.

All the little girls snap to attention, copying Elizabeth's funny salute. They're so serious about holding their breath, I hope Elizabeth puts her hand down before the group passes out.

This is such an Elizabeth moment. She's what she is, the perfect model of good behavior. And the bony-shouldered little girls looking up at her? They're like her, too. Happy to be good. Happy always to be steered left and right, sure of their eternal reward. And it's as if I'm watching from a shadow.

I stare too long, and Elizabeth finally feels my eyes on her.

She flushes and her hands fall to her sides. On impulse, I hustle toward her.

"That was great. You were always so good with kids," I say. "They adore you already."

"Oh. Thanks. Why are you here?" she asks cautiously.

"I'm supposed to be your babysitting partner," I say.

Just then, Sister Cecilia Alice opens the inner doors to the church and invites everyone inside. Father Waters, waiting near a pew full of wicker baskets, gestures for Elizabeth and me to come near.

"Hi, girls," he says. Then he asks me, "Isn't Jane here?"

When I tell him she's out of town, he says, "So you stepped up to the plate, Elizabeth?" And then he says to me, "It's nice to have old friends to depend on, right?"

I don't dare peek at Elizabeth.

Father tells us that we are to hand the baskets out to the first graders and instruct them on how to walk and throw flower petals at the same time. "Remember?" he says. "It's harder than it looks!" He winks. "Why don't you show them how it's done?"

When Elizabeth and I were here in little white communion dresses and veils, baskets full of petals from the florist, we had to be careful to take one step, bring a petal to our lips, kiss, and drop. Step, lift, kiss, and drop while the big girls sang, "Mary, we crown thee with flowers today."

"Mary Margaret," says Elizabeth, as if she's challenging me, "do you have your imaginary basket ready?"

"I have it right here."

"Ready? Begin," she says.

120

Father Waters starts—"Mary, we crown thee . . ."—in his booming tenor.

"Step! Lift! KISS and drop!" proclaims Elizabeth.

I fall in step down the aisle, waltzing until "KISS and drop!" starts to sound to my ears like an accusation. Or does Elizabeth just make me extra paranoid?

When the first graders seem confident, Sister has the entire group practice together. She blows on her pitch pipe, and the big girls begin.

The voices grow stronger as the little girls step in rhythm. Imaginary petals are being tossed reverently down the center aisle. It's mystical.

"Do you remember?" I say to Elizabeth as we watch from the back of the church.

"Yes," she says. "Just think, we've done first grade and eighth grade. The next time one of us walks down the aisle like this . . ."

I swallow hard and try not to let anything show.

"Will Paula wear your confirmation dress?" Elizabeth asks.

"No question," I say. "And probably Katie, too."

"I've still got my dopey one," Elizabeth says. It was something she got handed down from a bridesmaid cousin: unfashionably full skirted and, worse, sleeveless!

The nuns were maniacs about sleeveless dresses because they showed bra straps and gave boys "ideas." So Mrs. Healy went out and tried to match fabric, settling for not-quite-coordinating nylon-striped sheer sleeves. It turned out to be sort of the Frankenstein of confirmation gowns.

"Oh, Elizabeth," I say. "I'm surprised you kept it."

121

"Why?" she asks.

"Because! I remember you being all blubbery. I kept handing you Kleenex. It was like a big crisis, you wearing that dress."

Elizabeth turns cold. "Oh, please."

"Don't tell me you don't remember," I say.

Elizabeth turns to watch the procession. "That's so like you," she says. "Always making me out to be the neurotic."

I'm flustered. "But you were crying that day. I'm sure of it."

"But not over the stupid dress," says Elizabeth. She turns to me. "David got his draft notice that day. We weren't supposed to talk about it because . . ."

"No, David wasn't drafted until June," I say.

"We weren't supposed to tell anyone he was drafted," Elizabeth continues firmly, "because my parents didn't want him to go. He was supposed to go to Canada, Mary Margaret. With Dad. It was a secret."

"*Your father* was going to help Dave dodge the draft?" This is unthinkable. Mr. Healy, as far as I know, is still for the war.

"Yes. It was killing him. It still does."

"But he's super-patriotic, isn't he?"

"Now that Dave's over there, my dad's behind him. But it still kills him."

I'm silent for a few moments. "Elizabeth, if you had told me, I would have supported you. Completely. Why didn't you tell me?"

"Dave decided to go," she says simply. "And there's nothing for any of us to do except pray. And be good."

"Be good?"

"I made this pact with God. And I am going to do whatever I need to keep it. Whatever it costs."

"Or what?" I ask. "Something will happen to Dave?"

"I made a promise," she says, crossing her heart. "And believe it or not, I am tough enough to keep it."

I do understand. Being good really is the only thing she can do. And she has a bond with Dave like I have with Paula. Plus she's so, so Catholic.

"I'm sorry," I say. "For not being there for you."

"You didn't know," Elizabeth says.

"I should have tried harder to find out what was bothering you." She doesn't argue with that.

When practice is over, we collect the wicker baskets from the girls and put them in the storeroom. Elizabeth picks up her sweater and book bag, and as we head out, she says, "Walk me home?"

And I start to say yes when . . .

Honk!

Mitch is in his parents' car. He waves at me.

Elizabeth widens her eyes and, blushing deeply, turns her back to the car.

"Um," I say, cringing, "I already have a ride. But maybe, would you like a lift?"

"I'll walk, thanks," she says quickly.

"Oh, come on, Elizabeth. Let us drop you off. It's the least we can—"

Elizabeth raises her left hand and touches her right hand to her nose. I immediately stop talking.

"Works, doesn't it?" she says. Then, with a nod, she says, "Have fun, Mary Margaret."

"I will," I say dumbly. "You too." And I walk to Mitch's car feeling like the biggest creep.

But my fun and Elizabeth's fun are two different things. On our last day of school, Jane brings vodka and lemonade in a plaid thermos.

"My parents restocked the liquor cabinet," she says. "Let's celebrate."

We sit on the outdoor tables. She fills the plastic cup and pushes it toward me. "Drink up," she says.

Elizabeth is over at another table, but Constance and Kathy are only three feet away. Slowly I sip, trying not to choke. When I try to speak, my voice is hoarse. "How much actual lemonade is in here?"

"A sprinkle," says Jane. Then, whispering, she adds, "Don't worry. Vodka doesn't smell up your breath." She takes the cup, fills it, slugs it down, and licks her lips.

We do this back and forth. I feel swoony. When the final cup is drunk, Jane slams it down and squeals, "Is everybody happy?"

I cover my smile and snort. Constance and Kathy give us confused looks.

"What is it with her hair today?" Jane says, as if Constance can't hear. "She looks like old Rose Marie on *The Dick Van Dyke Show*."

Kathy visibly elbows Constance.

"Shhhhhh!" I say, trying to raise my finger to my mouth, which seems to have moved.

Sloppily happy during our final sweltering hours in the classroom, I stare cross-eyed at the catechism word-search puzzle Sister has given us.

Jane, though, sticks out her tongue and applies herself. I'm thinking she must have an ungodly high tolerance for alcohol when she hands me her work.

Circled are the words *dam, shit, whore, poop,* and *buggger.*

"What's *buggger?*" I ask.

"It's a sexual thing," Jane says, "which Sister obviously doesn't know how to spell."

When school's out, Jane hands the puzzle to Constance, who looks down and slowly crumples it. "You're drunk, aren't you?"

"Drunk on life," Jane says.

"It's possible, you know," I say smugly. Then I stick out my tongue. Constance is such a *buggger.*

Jane and I weave-skip-dance home, holding hands by the pinkie fingers, singing, "My baby does the hanky-panky . . . ," sort of showing the world how much more trouble we mean to get in.

Then I feel someone grab my other hand.

"Can we dance with you?" Paula asks. Katie is clinging to her side.

"Why not?" says Jane. She hops over and gives Paula a ballroom twirl.

"Me!" says Katie. So I twirl her, too.

"Kick line!" Jane puts her arm through mine and kicks like a chorus girl as Katie giggles. Jane kicks more violently. The barrettes start sliding from her hair.

"I can see her underwear," Katie says to Paula. Then one of Jane's square-toed flats goes flying off above her head. Paula ducks. It almost beans her.

As I fetch Jane's shoe, I realize that we've gone from being cool drunk to stupid drunk. With super-sober Constance and Kathy watching us, I'm struck by how Katie and Paula might see us.

"Okay, little sisters," I say, "run along home. I'll catch up."

"Awwwwww . . ."

"Now, don't fret. You'll see more of me this summer," Jane says.

"They've seen plenty enough of her already," I hear Constance say.

Deep down, I know she has a point, but then I'm suddenly distracted from my guilt by a monster case of the hiccups. My shoulders keep heaving up to my ears.

Jane puts her hand to my forehead. "Out, demons!" she says.

Our obnoxiousness finally drives Constance and Kathy to the other side of the street. "Good riddance," Jane says. "No more of them for three whole months. Just you and me!"

"I can *hic!* hardly wait," I say.

15

Actually, for the first weeks of summer, I don't even see Jane. I mean to see her, but there's Mitch. She's called me at least four times, and I've turned her down.

When I finally drop by, she says, "You're very new to all the sex stuff, and if you're completely blindsided for a while, that's to be expected. I hope you're enjoying yourself."

I watch as she folds her hands in her lap, perfectly accepting.

"Do you hate me?" I ask.

"No, you're fine. Of course, you'd have been better off if you'd waited for a Rainbow House guy. Should I bother to go on?"

"Jane, I don't know how to get this through to you. Mitch IS a Rainbow House guy. Potentially. And he'll be there with me, all summer."

"Hmmm. Well, I'm taking a break from regular life, anyway. I don't mind being alone."

She's been teaching herself how to play the guitar, writing

in her diary, reading and rereading *Siddhartha*. She has made Saturday pilgrimages to the Rainbow House just to listen while Donnie speaks. Last Friday, she took the bus to the house in the evening, only to find nobody there. She tells me how she sat on the doorstep a long time, just hanging around. Then, before she left, she went in the unlocked back door and cleaned his room.

"Dear God, that's so strange," I tell her. "And momlike. Is that what you want?"

"I'm learning how to serve," Jane says.

He hasn't even kissed her yet. Her response to his lack of response is to become more and more nunnishly self-sacrificing. Like Elizabeth? This isn't what we planned.

What's funny to me is that all this "lonely life" is new to her and that she likes it. My misery days of diary writing and lying around listening to music with tears dribbling from my eyes aren't far enough behind for me.

I just want to get in the car with Mitch every chance I can. He's been volunteering to do more errands, grocery shopping, anything. He comes by, honks, and picks me up. And every time, my mother makes a little gesture, like tossing down her dish towel and hissing through her teeth.

"Be right back!" I always say, sprinting out before she can question me.

We quickly pick up things at Piggly Wiggly, then park behind the One-Hour Cleaners and madly make out.

"Hallinan," he said once, coming up for air, "did you have any, like, hobbies before you met me? Any other . . . interests?"

"Nothing worth reporting."

"None? With any other guys?"

"None. Honestly," I told him. "You are the first. The only."

He nodded. "Good," he said, and went back to kissing my neck. Then he stopped. "Not that I own you or anything."

"Of course," I said, wishing Jane could hear how evolved Mitch really is. "Every time I kiss you, it's an act of complete free will. I am your all-volunteer make-out girl."

And now I'm losing part of my lower face. The constant abrasion of going at it has me peeling around the mouth and chin. I try Pond's cold cream, which helps at first, then gives me zits.

No, I'm not "dating." But I do have a plum-colored hickey on my collarbone that I can barely cover up with my hair, Maybelline foundation, and a buttoned-up blouse.

School's been out a couple of Sundays, but for the first time, Mitch's family and mine are both at the eleven o'clock mass. The Dunns usually go at eight. Anyway, I'm happily watching him sit, stand, and kneel when I get a heavy whiff of gardenia perfume. It's Mrs. Stephens and Jane! Mrs. Stephens is in fluttering false eyelashes and a sleeveless (!) Pucci shift. Jane is wearing a ton of beads and the shortest skirt this church has ever seen.

"Got room for my pagan butt?" Jane whispers. My mother growls, "Oh dear God," as I scoot down and let them in.

"I know," Jane says to me just as we start reciting the Apostles' Creed. "It's hypocritical. But Mom thinks we have to put in an appearance at least once in a while."

My mother hears this and starts praying louder. Dad notices and looks at her like, *What's with the volume?*

WE'RE THE REAL CATHOLICS! NOT LIKE YOU! she seems to be announcing. *YOU ARE AN AFFRONT TO THE LORD!*

I'm thinking that Mother will at least chat with Barbara Stephens after mass, but she only says a quick hello, grabs my father's hand, and drags him outside. She barely waits for us kids.

"I don't know what she's up to," I say, trying to spare Mrs. Stephens's feelings. "Maybe she's getting Daniel from the nursery."

"See ya round later?" says Jane.

"Of course!" I say.

Katie, Paula, and Kevin follow me outside.

"There's Mommy!" says Katie, pointing.

Dad's by her side, and she's shaking hands with Mr. and Mrs. Dunn. Mitch's brother Matt is there, too.

"Oh no." I grab Katie's hand and hustle over there as fast as I can. By the time I've joined them, Mitch's mom is eyeing me suspiciously.

"So, you are Mitchell's girlfriend?" Mrs. Dunn says to me. I wait for Mitch.

"Mary Margaret and me, yeah," says Mitch, shifting from foot to foot. "We're good friends."

"Yes, indeed," says my mom. "We see Mitch at our place all the time. Or at least we hear him honking. Once he even came all the way to the door. Right, Don?"

Dad nods. "Yep."

Mitch's dad, a big guy with a gray and strawberry blond crew cut, says, "Is that where you're taking the Impala four times a day?"

"Yes, sir," Mitch says stonily. "Sometimes. When I'm in her neighborhood or whatnot."

Matt, a big working guy like his father, twists his mouth to keep from laughing.

"I see," says Mitch's mom, narrowing her eyes. "Well, of course it's nice to meet you . . ."

"Mary Margaret," I say.

"Mary Margaret," she repeats slowly, as if she intends to keep my name filed under *Potential Hussy.*

Mother and Dad say goodbye, and all is quiet until we're back in the station wagon with the doors closed.

"Could you believe that boy, Don?"

"What about him?" my father says wearily.

"Mother," I interrupt, "tell me what you said to the Dunns!"

"You hold your horses," Mom shoots back at me. "I don't know what kind of crowd you're running with now, but that was an inexcusably rude exchange."

"Mitch's folks were not rude!" I say.

"Not them. That boy." She turns to my dad again. "That boy wouldn't even acknowledge her," Mom continues. "His 'good friend.' Good enough to pick up for a joyride."

"What's a joyride?" asks Katie.

"That boy is ashamed of you, Mary Margaret," Mother says. She folds her arms. "And I have to wonder if you've given him reason to be."

131

"Cynthia," Dad pleads. "Don't you think you're jumping to conclusions? He's just a kid."

"A nice young man," my mother enunciates, "does not take a girl out in his car for one-hour trips and disown her in front of his parents."

"Aw, this talk is making me sick," Kevin says, plugging his ears.

"A nice young man," continues my mother, "does not disown a girlfriend in front of her father, either. Unless he has absolutely no respect for her or her family."

"It's not like that, Mother!" I say.

"AND that Jane!" Mother says to Dad. "How many boys are honking their horns for their one-hour turn at the Stephens girl?"

"What's so bad about honking horns?" Paula asks.

"*Nothing!*" I yell.

"Stop screamin'!" shouts Kevin, still plugging his ears.

"Was Daddy a nice young man?" I ask Mother. "Were you a nice young lady? How about THAT?"

As soon as my dad stops the car in the driveway, I yank open the door and run as fast as I can in a stupid garter belt and stockings.

"Mary Margaret!" my mother says. "Where do you think you're going?"

"I'm going," I say, "where people UNDERSTAND ME!" Then I see Mrs. Switzer in her housecoat, watering her grass and looking amazed, and I know how hysterical I sound.

"Goddammit," I whisper. I stop running and settle for a clunky walk.

16

When I get to Jane's, Mrs. Stephens actually throws her arms around me. "Well, look who's here!" she says. "We've missed Mary Margaret, haven't we, Avery?"

Mr. Stephens looks up from the table strewn with books and legal pads and nods distractedly.

"I just saw you a few minutes ago," I say.

"Yes, but not at the house. Jane has been funny lately," says Mrs. Stephens confidentially, leading me down the hall. "Visits that Rob a lot. You know Rob?"

"Yeah," I say. "He's nice. If you're worried, I mean."

Mrs. Stephens hangs back, checking my expression. "Good to hear," she says. "We know the family, but you still wonder. Though I must say, I'm glad to see you back. Solid girl!" She smiles.

"Yeah, that's me," I say.

We stop at Jane's door. She's listening to the Beatles. "Darling, you have company!" Mrs. Stephens sings.

"Enter!"

My first urge is to plop down on the floor with her and tell her every detail of what happened with Mitch since I saw her last. But she starts speaking quickly.

"Did you pass the Gargoyle?" Jane asks.

"Huh?"

"*Avery*, stupid!"

"Uh, I walked by," I say.

"I hate it when he brings work home on the weekends. He hangs around the house and takes up all the oxygen. I wish he'd go out and get in a car accident."

"Jane!"

"I'm just saying how I feel," she says. "I have to stay in my room all day whenever Avery's here. But it's either that, or . . . really, I might just kill him myself." She breathes in and out, picks up her copy of *Siddhartha*, and fans herself with it. "Guess that wasn't very spiritual, was it?"

"Probably not," I say.

"Anyway, this book? It's spooky," she declares. "There are so many things I've been aware of all along but I didn't know that I knew. You know?"

I sit on Jane's carpet. *Revolver*'s on the stereo.

> She said, "You don't understand what I
> said."
> I said, "No, no, no, you're wrong. . . ."

"For instance, Siddhartha. Like me, he instinctively knows how to influence people. It's no big deal to him because he was born with this gift. But he's trying to get at something more, some meaning. And he takes all these paths. . . ." Jane lowers her gaze. "Am I boring you?"

Actually, I am a little bored. "Go on," I say.

"One of the paths is sex, Mary Margaret," Jane says. "SEX." She knocks on my forehead.

"Ouch," I say.

"Okay. Your turn. Speaking of sex . . ."

Finally. "Good and not good," I tell her. "I'm thinking maybe I'm getting in over my head? And then I love getting in over my head."

"Sounds normal, if that's what you're asking."

I tell her, dead serious: "I'm afraid of doing it."

"Oh, Mary Margaret."

"I could do it in, like, a second."

"So?"

"So, do you ever get that feeling when the garbage disposal is running? You're afraid you're going to jam your hand right down there. Even though you'll spend the rest of your life with a bloody stump, the urge is practically irresistible."

"If by *bloody stump*, you mean *Mitch*," Jane says, "you might be onto something."

"All right. That's the last time I want to hear you bad-mouth him. Doesn't it mean anything that *I* like him? And another thing, Jane: *he* gets me."

"Are you saying I don't?" Jane asks.

"Of course not. I'm only trying to make you understand."

Jane sighs, closes her eyes. "I'm sorry," she says, "but can

135

I tell you what I'm seeing? You like Mitch because you like taking care of somebody. You're that kind of girl."

"What kind of girl are you, then?" I ask.

"I don't want to take care of a boy. I want to be an *inspiration*."

"Then what the hell are you cleaning his room for?"

"Because, Mary Margaret, *that* is new to *me*! It's more a symbolic thing, anyway." Then, almost to herself, she adds, "The sad part about actual sex is it's probably not going to be as earth-shattering as you think."

"How can you say that?"

Jane sits still and gives me a compassion-of-Jesus look. "What can I say? Sex can be a dead end. But at the end of the book, Siddhartha is glad he's tried everything. He doesn't know regret."

"Just like you," I stab back.

"Sort of." She bites the inside of her lip. "At least I do try not to regret."

I roll over on my back. It's not right, bickering like this. "Let's talk about you, then. Are you through with your sex phase?"

"What a weird thought," she says. "Aren't I too young to be through? I don't even think my parents are through. Especially Avery. The pervert."

Jane can't know how carefully I shield myself from parental-sex thoughts, especially since my mother is procreating. I visibly shudder.

"Oops, sorry," says Jane. "Anyway. I don't seem to be able

to completely empty myself out and give. Donnie says it's not good to always have to be in charge."

"Now wait a minute," I say. "When your old boyfriend, Ronald—"

"Roger," says Jane.

"When Roger betrayed you and ran off that night and left you with your butt still hanging out your bedroom window, you weren't in charge."

"Roger was a jerk."

"He sold you out to your parents."

"He was a coward," Jane says.

"Jane, you should be looking for somebody to stand by you," I say.

She places her hand on her book. "There are probably at least one thousand and seventy-nine paths to love and enlightenment, and we all have our own ways. Mine is just different from yours, maybe from anyone's." She squints. "And don't think I'm an ass."

"You are not an ass," I tell her. "And I'm not, either, for picking Mitch."

"Mary Margaret, you're the one person I trust to put up with me. I'm trying so hard. At something. For once."

I roll over on my stomach and catch her nakedly worried face. "Jane, I'm sorry. Just, please . . ."

"What?"

"Don't stop being funny. I depend on you for that. For laughs."

"Poor Mary Margaret. My funny IS missing lately, isn't it?"

"Hey," I say, "don't you remember how you used to say it was worthless for women to try to get men to take them seriously?"

"I did." Jane halts me with her hand. "But Donnie's different. And I've changed."

We decide to walk to Dairy Queen so we can smoke. Once we're out of Jane's neighborhood, there are lawns full of whirling plastic sunflowers, hand-painted mailboxes, and burlwood signs announcing THE COONEYS! BOB, DONNA, DEBBIE, JON, AND PATCHES!

A few months ago, I'd have walked past all this without a thought. Now I automatically picture having a sign made like that for me and Mitch and our squalling babies and our depressed dog. I'm immediately nauseated.

"Do you ever look around and think we're surrounded by false advertising for everybody's happiness?"

"Always," Jane says.

"I don't know that I ever saw that till I met you."

Jane squeezes my arm. "So I've made you aware and unhappy."

"Not unhappy," I tell her. "Without you, I'd never even have tried to get to know Mitch. Or noticed how much people try to scare you. Like, happiness must be avoided at all costs for the sake of society or something. So we're supposed to agree to be satisfied with this dead, horrible substitute."

"Yes! Never settle. That's my motto!"

"Right on!"

"Because I believe in happiness." She gestures to the sky. "Above all else."

We walk along in silence for a while. "Let's go to the Rainbow House," I finally say.

"You got bus money?" she asks.

"Right now?"

"Yeah! Now!" She takes my hand. "We'll go, stay a minute, turn around, come back."

As if by command, a Sunday express bus comes rumbling up behind us on San Rafael Boulevard.

"Karma!" says Jane.

"Fate!" I say. I hop across a fried lawn, drop my cigarette into an imitation wishing well, and run back to the bus stop.

"The world is our ashtray, darling," says Jane. She throws her cigarette over her shoulder, and we skip our way up the stairs of the waiting bus.

17

I've never been to the Rainbow House in broad daylight. The door is unlocked, and we don't knock. There's the aroma of coffee and marijuana smoke in the air, the sound of Rob picking on his acoustic guitar in the kitchen. And though the furniture's busted and everything's worn, I'm surprised the place is so comfy.

"Could we live like this?" I say to Jane. "You and me. Someday?"

"You and me and whoever," says Jane. "Sure."

We make our way up the stairway to Donnie's room. Nobody's there.

"Let's sit and wait," Jane says, plopping on the perfectly made bed.

"Man, Jane, you must have cleaned your butt off in here." The place is laboratory-neat, with magazines shelved according to size and cheap furniture lined up at precise right angles.

"Actually," Jane says, "this is how it looks all the time. Donnie says that clutter in 'his space' clutters his consciousness."

"So what did you do here?"

"Um, just straightened the pillows and dusted the place with my underwear."

"Jane! Ew."

"I threw them away afterward."

We hear a toilet flush, and then Donnie appears at the door. "Janey," he states coolly. Is he ever surprised?

"Hey," says Jane. "Glad to see me?" I can tell she's straining not to seem giddy.

He doesn't answer, just leans against the door frame.

"I'm sorry," she says. "I know I'm not supposed to ask."

"Jane," says Donnie, "you are free to ask anything you like. Just as I'm free to answer only when I choose."

She beams at him. I glare.

"We won't be here long," she says.

"Understood," he says. He enters the room, sits on a stool, bends over his desk, and pulls a plastic bag of pot from the drawer. We watch him roll a joint in respectful silence.

I notice how he lines everything up on the desk: the papers, the bag, the kitchen matches. He makes every move seem like part of a ceremony.

My nose itches. I scratch it. I tap my foot. For some reason, my body just won't keep still.

Donnie pauses. Stares.

I stop squirming. Then he goes back to licking the paper.

"Ever since I was little," I explain, "I never fidget unless I'm not supposed to fidget."

"And what do you think," Donnie asks without looking up, "that says about you?"

"I never thought about it," I say.

"I think," says Jane, "it means Mary Margaret is uncomfortable with stillness outside herself."

"Very good, Janey," Donnie says approvingly. "Most people think the challenge is to remain still when there's surrounding chaos. But actually, it's just as strict a discipline to remain still when others are quiet." He pauses, then pronounces, "Go placidly amidst the noise and haste . . . and also the *stillness*."

What in the world does Jane see in this guy? Besides his face and fab body, I mean.

"Maybe that's why church is so hard on me," Jane says. "Hmmm. I never thought I could use the time in mass for *real* spiritual work."

"What are you talking about?" I say. "If people aren't doing real spiritual work in church, then what are they doing?"

Donnie barely smiles. "That's a deep question."

"It is," Jane agrees.

"Are you going to light up that joint, or are we going to contemplate it in *stillness?*" I say.

Donnie, unbothered, slooowly strikes the match, lights the joint, inhales. I reach for it, and he leaves me waiting for a long time. When I finally take my second hit, the anger in me seems to deflate. It occurs to me that the only way I could be around Donnie for any length of time is to be high, high, high.

"I'm gonna go downstairs and find Rob."

He's on the phone.

I watch his lips talk on the phone.

"Heyyyy," says Gordon. He and Van are sitting on the floor, leaning against the kitchen cabinets.

"Oh my God! I didn't see you there."

"What's happenin', little sister? You look like you're dressed up for Sunday school."

"Mass, actually," I say.

Gordon, Van, and I wait, watching Rob like he's a TV show until he puts the phone down. "I take it someone wants to make a call?" he says.

"Could you call a number for me?" I ask.

"You can call yourself if you want!" He grins.

"No, no. I can't call because I don't want to talk to Mitch's parents. I need a guy voice."

"Gordon has a hypnotic voice," Van says. "Put him on the phone with anyone, and they will do your bidding."

Gordon inhales. "Why, Van," he says, holding his breath. "What a lovely thing to say."

Gordon takes the receiver while I dial. "Mitch there?" he says. "Mitchy? Mitcherooni? That you?" I grab the phone.

"Who the hell is this?" says Mitch's voice.

"It's me. Mary Margaret," I say.

"What? Who's the other guy?"

"I got Gordon to call because I'm too embarrassed to talk to your parents."

"Oh yeah," says Mitch. "Listen. I know. . . ."

"My mom is just so . . . she's nosy and embarrassing."

"Really? I thought *I* was embarrassing. It must look like I don't want to be with you. When it's just the opposite. Your folks must think I'm a jerk."

"You are not a jerk."

"Thanks. You're not a jerk, too."

"Oh, Mitchell, your voice sounds so good. I'm glad you're home." He asks if I want to meet him. Somewhere he won't have to borrow the car.

"There's the bus stop by the golf course," I say. "I could be there in an hour."

"Yeah, me too. I wanna see you."

"I wanna see you, too. I am leaving right this second." I put down the phone without saying goodbye and run to tell Jane.

I can't believe what I see when I stand in Donnie's doorway. Donnie is sitting in his chair, just as I last saw him. And Jane? Her shirt is hiked up, revealing the long line of her backbone, and she's straddling him like a cowgirl. Donnie's head is bent back and she's kissing him.

" 'Scuse me," I say.

She looks up, sees me, and gives me this victorious smile. Donnie turns and catches me looking, then says in his no-big-deal voice: "In or out?"

"Leaving," I say.

Shudder. They're so wrong together somehow. I want to tell her to wear a crash helmet. It seems obvious to me that

144

this is something that isn't going to be good for Jane, whatever it is.

I actually run to the bus stop, feeling my Romeo-Juliet feeling. I'm secretly meeting the guy and my parents are mad and I don't really care because I am so happy. And he's just as into me as I am to him.

I begin a prayer. *Thank you, God, for making my wish come true. Thank you for giving me the boy I wanted. I never thought I'd have him for my own.* And then, maybe it's the pot, but I start thinking about whether Mitch and I will last. If we don't, will I be the one who gets clobbered?

The golf course comes into view, and I see him there in the dusk looking up for me, and only me, but I'm somewhere in between. My heart is busting, but my mind has pulled back, watching.

Mitch takes my hand and helps me to the curb.

"Don't think you have to be a gentleman now," I say. "My mother can't see you."

He's quizzical. "So?" he says.

"I mean, you know, today . . . I understand you weren't going to let them stamp BOYFRIEND on your butt. My feelings aren't really hurt."

"So . . . ," he says, waiting.

"So let's not change who we are for them. I like you the way you are."

"All right, all right," Mitch says. "Sometimes, though, I don't know what you want. I'm not always trying to be 'different.' I don't always want to be thinking. I'm just doing what I feel. Okay?"

"Hmmm. And what would you feel like doing? Right now?" I ask.

Mitch cocks his head and smiles, and I'm not going to act dumb.

I lead him to a patch of untended land behind the parking lot overlooking the seventh hole, another place where Jane and I go for smokes. Farther out, the grass comes up to my rib cage. We walk until we can't see the cars.

"Find me!" Mitch holds his arms straight out on either side and falls straight back into the weeds. He disappears.

"Ha!" I throw off my shoes, pull down my garter belt, and peel off my fishnet stockings. Then I spread my arms and do the same. The foxtail is so thick, it breaks my fall like a mattress.

"You find me!" I shout.

I hear him burrowing through the long weeds. I lie looking up at the pale stars, then spring up and grab Mitch as he passes through. He falls on top of me and we roll around like we're playing King of the Hill. Then we're back at it again.

Since I've been with Mitch, we've been pushing clothes out of the way, hands over and under, without taking anything off. It's less sinful as long as I do it with my clothes on. But part of me always wants Mitch to unbutton something. Tonight I sit up, trying to make it easier for him to undo my bra. I bite his earlobe as his hand travels up my back. After what seems to be five minutes of pinches and elastic snappings—unshackled!

He puts his hand to my collar, unbuttons one button,

then stops. "Is this okay?" he says, so meltingly sweet. "Should I?"

"You should," I say, placing a finger on his lips. "But first . . ."

"What?"

I swallow hard. "But first, Mitchell, I want you to show me your leg."

Mitch lowers his chin defensively.

"Let me tell you why," I say quickly. "Because if I take off my shirt and you'll get to see my, you know . . . it's the exact same thing. It'll make us even."

Mitch sits up, puts his hand on his bum knee, and thinks. "I don't want to," he says finally.

I take his face in my hands. "You gotta be scared, too," I say. "And you gotta trust me. Then I'll trust you."

I kiss him just once, hoping he can feel everything I'm putting into it: friendship and tenderness and lust. Then I pull back and wait.

"Aw, shit!" he says. Then he stands, determined, like he's about to rip off a Band-Aid. He undoes his belt, unzips his cords, and lets them fall to his skinny ankles. I'm amazed at what I see.

His one beautiful leg, the normal one, is so muscled it could have been made with a chisel. Maybe that's because he works it twice as hard. The other leg is withered at the calf and big at the knee. My eyes spring full of tears.

"My sweetheart," I say. "My Mitch." I drop to my knees and wrap my arms around both legs. I kiss each knee. When

I stand again, I whisper in his ear, "I love all of you. Every inch. I just do."

"Your turn," he says softly. He unbuttons me and I shrug off my blouse. We fall down and the grass is scratchy. I pull his T-shirt up into a tangle under his armpits. I watch the change of expression on his face as he bares his teeth, tears his shirt over his head, and throws it.

All of his weight is on top of me, and I feel an insistent prodding on my upper thigh. Now the earth pounds with choirs of frogs and crickets. Tear me limb from limb? Feed me to the wolves? I'm unharmable, and every sensation is good.

"Shhh!" hisses Mitch, paralyzed.

I clear my head, and suddenly I can hear it, too. The gravel crunches. A car is slowing down nearby.

"Don't move," Mitch whispers. A radio is crackling. "It's either a taxicab or a cop." When a harsh white light strobes over the grass, we have our answer.

"Anybody out here? Police!"

I start flailing around for my blouse. Where *is* it? Oh my God.

"Keep still!" whispers Mitch.

There's a stirring in the grass. *Oh Lord Jesus,* I pray. Silently I let him know how sincerely ashamed I am, a naked girl outdoors, a topless little slut.

Mitch clutches me around the shoulders as the light comes closer. I'm shaking in terror as the giant flashlight bears down on us, bright as a laser.

"Stand up."

"I—I can't," I stutter.

"I said stand up. Both of you."

"Here." Mitch mercifully pitches his T-shirt to me, and I drape it across my chest and clamp it with my elbows. We stand side by side, like two half-dressed suspects in a criminal lineup, definitely guilty and caught red-handed.

"Young lady, are you all right?"

"Yes, Officer," I say. I can see now that the cop isn't alone. His backup has a hand on his holster. He may as well kill me and get it over with.

"Look," says Mitch, pulling up his pants, "can we just step over here and let this girl get dressed?"

They ignore him and take our names. They ask Mitch for his license. They lecture us about private-property rights. I'm picturing myself behind bars, braless and in a boy's T-shirt, waiting for my father to pick me up from jail.

"Normally," says the cop, "we'd call your parents. But if you get yourselves together and go right home, we'll let it go. Just this once."

I hurry up and stuff my stockings in my bra. When we're dressed, they escort us to the street.

The backup cop looks over his shoulder and gives me his parting shot. "Damn lucky you're not my daughter, little girl," he says.

Mitch and I start walking. "You hear that?" I ask him. "Taunting me, like I'm the only one in trouble. Blame the girl."

Mitchell keeps his eyes on the road ahead. "I'm really sorry, Mary Margaret."

"Me too," I tell him. "Why don't they call *you* 'little boy'? I am so pissed. I could've punched him in the mouth!"

"I should have done way more. I'm really . . . I feel like shit."

"Stop. You can't really punch a cop in the mouth." What I'm thinking is, *Why can't I be the kind of person who gets away with things?* After a long silence, I say, "It's all very Adam and Eve, isn't it? Stupid Eve."

He doesn't need this statement explained. He's had ten years of Catholic school.

When I walk in the house, I'm stockingless, I've missed dinner, and I'm a tiny bit high.

My dad is dishing out bowls of ice cream for an evening of *Walt Disney's Wonderful World of Color.*

"Glad you're back," he says simply, and hands me a bowl of ice cream.

There's something to be said for certain kinds of parental obliviousness. I duck his gaze, put my arm around his waist, and bury my face in his shoulder.

18

Unlike Jane, who spends her time mooning all alone in penthouse-type splendor, I am my mother's summer slave. She keeps me busy doing all sorts of chores. I have to go to U-Pick and get berries for jam, which Paula and I then have to make and put up.

"You aren't talking very much," Paula says as she spoons sugar into a pot of hot strawberries.

"It's too hot to talk," I say. But I'm really just going over and over my last evening with Mitch. Little bits of him—the blond on his forearms, his freckled shoulder, the line of his jaw—flash before my eyes whenever I blink. Even if I tried, I couldn't stop this constant replay. My brain and heart are swamped with him, and it must show.

"I heard you can tell how a boy is your destiny," Paula says.

"Really." I stir busily. "How?"

"When you kiss, you hear bells. That's what Annie Row-
ley says." Paula tilts her head and goes swoony. "When you
kiss Mitch, do you hear them?"

"Nope. Don't hear a thing."

"Then maybe he's not your true love," Paula says. "Do
you think he's your true love?"

I take a pair of tongs and pull a jelly jar out of the pan of
boiling-hot water. "True love," I repeat. "I guess I'm not
sure."

Paula slumps. I'm disappointing her.

"I promise," I say. "If I ever hear bells, I'll tell you. I'll
keep my ears open."

Love, or whatever it is I'm feeling, isn't light and jingly.
It's raging in my bloodstream like a fever. I just cannot talk to
Paula about that.

Mitch and his two older brothers visit his grandparents'
ranch every summer. He'll be back on Friday. My mother
takes my being around as an opportunity to get out of the
house, leaving me to babysit the kids. I haven't had a chance
to run through a sprinkler, let alone go to the Rainbow
House.

On Thursday afternoon, Jane calls me. She's all pan-
icked. Her parents are going out of town for a cousin's wedding and they're going to take her along.

"Please, please let me stay with you," she says. "They're
trying to take me to Boise. As in Idaho."

"Land of the potato," I say, drawling like a cowboy.

"I can't be away from Donnie."

"But Mitch is coming home on Friday night. I want to see him, too."

"Oh, come on, Mary Margaret! Are you really going to make me go to Idaho? How many times have you stayed at MY house?"

It's no accident that I've kept Jane at a distance from my home life. I've told myself that it's because I want to be part of her world and that she wouldn't get anything out of mine—especially with my mother's raging. Who knows what she might say to Jane? Overall, I'm a little ashamed. I picture Paula and Katie, my poor little sisters, and our squished-together room. Our one toilet and dingy bathtub. I know I shouldn't, and I hate myself for caring about stuff like this.

"Gee, I haven't had anybody sleep over since Elizabeth," I tell her. "We had to pitch a pup tent in the backyard."

"So," says Jane, "I can sleep in a pup tent."

"Really?"

"It'll be great! We won't even have to wake anybody up when we come home."

"Okay. I'll ask my mom. But I warn you, it's a different world over here. You'll have babies crying and chores and no more than ten seconds to pee and brush your teeth."

"You exaggerate, sweetie."

"Oh no, sweetie. I don't."

When I ask if Jane can stay the weekend, Mother sighs deeply. "I'll say yes if, and only if, you two take care of breakfast both mornings. I can't wait on you and your friend."

"Pancakes," I say. "Bacon. Everything."

153

Jane arrives just in time for dinner on Friday. Afterward she helps me clear, scrape, and wash dishes.

"I don't get it," she says as she places the silverware in the sink. "Don't all these dirty dishes just get dirt on the other dishes?"

"That's what the soap is for."

"Yeah, but in a dishwasher, the plates are all cleaned more . . . separately." She pulls out a wet plate with her thumb and finger and lets it drip on the kitchen floor. "There's a smudge on this one."

I toss her the sponge. "Use this," I say.

The plate drops from her hand and bounces on the linoleum. She picks up the saucer and bangs it against the counter's edge. "It's some sort of miracle material."

"Cut it out," I say. "It's Melmac, but you can still break it."

"Oh. I'm sorry," she says, crumpling. "I really do think it's cool coming over here, seeing how you do things."

"Like visiting a different planet almost, I'll bet."

As we wait in line for the bathroom, I see Jane peer into Mother's room, where Paula is changing the baby for bed.

"Oh my God," she says. "You let her do that?"

I'm bugged. "Would you like a turn?"

"I might try it," she says, ignoring my irritation. "Why not?"

My father pushes to the front of the line and starts shouting at Kevin about power tools through the bathroom door.

"You weren't kidding. You're never alone here! Not even *in the bathroom!*"

Later I make popcorn on the stove and hand her a

pitcher from the fridge and two metal cups. "Pour us some Kool-Aid," I say to distract her from further "revelations" about our "lifestyle."

It's a genuine summer evening, warmish with the scent of neighborhood grilling. We lie on our sleeping bags outside and eat by flashlight.

"You know, Mary Margaret," says Jane, now sporting an orange Kool-Aid mustache, "you could be a pioneer woman. Really. You have survival skills. I had no idea."

"I always thought that you were the one with the serious skills. I'm just your faithful hick companion."

"No!" insists Jane. "Look at your place here. You're important in your family. It's, like, what would they do without you?"

"Give all my jobs to Paula," I say.

"What about Kevin?"

I think about this. Kevin doesn't babysit or change diapers, clean the table or fold laundry. Only once in a while does he help with dishes. "He mows the lawn. Sometimes he washes the car. Boy things," I say. "His job is to be Dad's pal, mostly."

"I tried that for a while," Jane says. "My real dad showed me how to make a martini when I was six. And so I made it my job after that to make his little cocktail every night and have it ready when he came home, and he'd sit on the couch and talk to me. After a week, he told me to stop."

"Well, I guess no parent wants a little-girl bartender."

Jane sets her jaw. "Oh, I'm sure Avery would just dig it if I made him martinis. He's so goony and excitable."

"Those are two words I'd never use for Avery," I say. "Isn't he kind of a stuffed shirt?"

"I wish he was stuffed and mounted."

"Why do you hate him so much?"

"Because," Jane states, "he married my mother right after Dad died. Like, *a minute* after. He was my dad's law partner, and I think Avery and my mom are to blame. It's this feeling I have."

"Jane, are you saying they had something to do with your dad dying?"

Her chin trembles, then she recovers. "If you're asking did they murder him," she says flatly, "then not precisely."

"That's not what I was asking," I say. Then softly, I say, "You never talk about your dad. It's hard for you, isn't it?"

Jane nods. "He killed himself."

I sense that Jane needs me to be matter-of-fact. "I guessed that," I say.

"Figured you did." Jane examines the ends of her hair.

"So the main reason you hate Avery is you think that he took your mother from your dad. . . ."

"Dad knew about the two of them, and he was already low. He was always high times and deep valleys, as my mother liked to say. But I remember he was low at the time." Jane leans forward, and I can see the lines of anguish on her forehead. "The last week he was alive, he came in every night and sat on the edge of my bed. Just sat there like he was watching me. And deciding, you know?"

"No. Tell me."

156

"He was trying to decide whether to *live*," Jane says. "Instead, he drove to Reno and shot himself in a parking lot."

I put my hand on her shoulder. "That's so, so awful. I'm sorry, Jane. So sorry."

She shrugs me off. "Don't be *sorry*. See, it's all worked out just peachy for my mother," Jane says. "She needs to be a fascinator. And I'm always in the way. As if I want to be anywhere near Avery. She's just so wrapped up in him. It's like there's no room for me."

"Wow." I always thought my life would be completely, wonderfully different if my parents were "wrapped up" with each other in a good way.

"Do you know," Jane says, "how happy my mom is that I'm staying here? Now they can be alone in the middle of nowhere in some hotel. And Avery won't be opening doors on me and following me around with his tongue hanging out."

"Be honest, Jane," I say. "Do you just hate Avery's guts in general or is he really coming on to you?"

"I'm not completely sure. Oh God. Nothing's happened," Jane says. "Let's change the subject. Please?"

"It's too hard to change the subject after talking like this," I say.

"Then let's do something that doesn't require any more talking." She folds her arms, and I can see there won't be any more on this topic.

"*Where the Boys Are* is the midnight movie," I offer. "Have you seen it?"

"Tons of times," Jane says. She explains that it concerns a bunch of not-so-cute boys and the four girls who go husband hunting during spring break in Fort Lauderdale, Florida.

"Everyone's deciding whether or not to lose their virginity. Guess how it ends," she says.

"With four weddings?"

"Noooooo," Jane says with a strange smile.

We decide to go and watch as the girls change outfits, do the Watusi, make out, change outfits. It's the kind of movie that we'd normally laugh at. But Jane and I are really quiet during the final scene, where the adorable, blond Yvette Mimieux has had so much sex with so many fraternity boys that she has a nervous breakdown and walks like the undead through heavy traffic in her underwear.

"This is the stupidest movie ever," I say.

"Oh, she'll be all right after a nice stay in a sanatorium."

"How? Does she take the cure for slut disease?"

"Ha ha. Guess what?" Jane says brightly. "There IS no cure for slut disease!" Jane stays quiet but still holds that strange smile.

"What?" I ask.

Jane's eyes sparkle as she squeezes my arm. "I did it. With Donnie!"

"When? Why didn't you tell me?"

"He was taking a nap in the afternoon, and the house was empty. This was two weeks ago. . . ."

"But I thought you were on a spiritual path."

"Oh. But we are!"

Jane describes how she'd come armed with her copy of *Siddhartha* and a necklace that she'd woven together with flowers and strands of her own hair. "Because," as she explains it, "I wanted to give him a part of me."

"Well, you certainly did that," I say. "God. I didn't think you guys were into that."

"We weren't. In fact, he woke up kind of grumpy and wasn't really in the mood to talk about anything. So I just waited on the edge of his bed while he fell back asleep. He's a beautiful sleeper."

Immediately my mind flashes on the scene of Jane's father waiting on the edge of her bed all those years ago. I'm chilled.

"Don't freak out," Jane says. "Anyway, I sat for a long time and meditated on his face and his body in bed. And then I took off my clothes and slipped on the necklace and crawled in with him between the sheets."

"Yes?"

"And he, as they say, *took me!*"

"How was it? How was he?"

"It was tender and mystical and . . . Our souls were like this." Jane presses her hands together and slowly intertwines her fingers. "Like they melted and joined."

I so want to believe her. "So it was everything you thought it could be. I'm glad."

"It was better than with Roger, let's just say."

"How was Donnie afterward?"

"It was so nice. After we were done, he just kissed me on the forehead. We didn't even say anything. I pulled on my shorts and my blouse and walked out smiling. We had a silent understanding."

"Really." With Mitchell and me, we're both hypnotized and intense as we wade into ever more treacherous currents. Noises come out of us—like rooting animals. Sex between Jane and Donnie, on the other hand, sounds like an airy, shifting dance between the controlling and the controlled.

"Did he say anything? Like *See you later*? Or *I love you?*"

"I already told you," Jane says impatiently, "we were silent. We didn't need words."

I press my lips together to avoid saying anything upsetting.

19

In the morning, after learning to flip pancakes, Jane makes enough for an army. When she runs out of batter, she makes another bowl. But she doesn't eat any herself. "More fun to make than to eat," she explains.

"Time to change gears, Jane," I tell her after breakfast. "We've got to stop cooking and start washing."

"I'll wash!" she says. "Don't help me!"

My mother, looking pleased at Jane's frenzied banging around, passes through just as the phone is ringing. "Hello?" she answers. Her face falls. "Yes, this is she."

The frosty way she speaks makes me assume it's a salesman until she hands the phone over and says, "It's that Mitchell."

I cover the receiver and wait for Mother to leave. She doesn't.

"Mary Margaret?"

"Hi," I say. "You're back!"

"What are you doing tonight?"

My mother, pretending to need a glass from a nearby cupboard, is definitely leaning in to listen.

"Well," I say, "Jane and I are GOING TO THE MOVIES. I'm sorry. It's a long story."

I hear him breathing.

"I guess I'll be seeing you after the weekend, then. Like I said, I'm really sorry."

"Yeah," he says.

"Is everything okay, Mitch?"

"You're not really going to Rob's tonight, are you? By yourself?"

"No, I'm going with Jane."

"Yeah, well . . . I gotta go. I'll try to talk to you later," he says. *Click.* He hangs up before I can say goodbye.

I look into the receiver.

"What does he want?" Jane asks.

"Me, I think," I say.

Mother makes her huffing sound and walks away.

"Finally she leaves," I say. "I should have asked Mitch to come with us. She got me all flustered with her obvious spying."

"I'd rather go with just you, anyhow," Jane says.

We are both antsy for a night out. When we get off the bus downtown, Jane removes her shoes, putting them in her bag. "I want to look exactly how I looked the last time I was in his bedroom," she says.

We walk up the splintered stairs to the porch, plunk down as if we belong, and wait for someone sympathetic we can ask for pot. Jane zeroes in on a twentyish guy with streaky hair, silver rings, and an embroidered belt and pulls the hem of his bell-bottoms.

"Hey," she says, "do you know where we can get some weed?"

He closes one eye. "How old are you?"

"I'm a friend of Donnie's," she says.

"Sure you are," he says. "You have papers?"

"No," says Jane, "I didn't bring any."

I'm thinking he wants to see our identification until, reluctantly, he takes a packet out of his pants pocket, pulls out a little white paper square, and starts rolling a joint for Jane.

"I can kick in for this, you know," says Jane.

"Dope doesn't grow on trees," he says. He licks the joint sealed and hands it to Jane. "Or maybe it does?"

"Thanks," she says. "How much do I owe you?"

"Nothing. Just don't tell anyone you got it from me," he says without a smile. "And don't ask me again."

Jane grins sweetly, says, "All righty," then as soon as the guy's out of sight gives him the finger. "Let's go share this with Donnie."

I notice the house feels different tonight. The music isn't as loud. More people are sitting around talking. I follow Jane up to the landing outside Donnie's door. She knocks.

"Who is it?" Donnie shouts.

Jane looks at me, flushed and happy, and gives the doorknob a twist. It's locked.

She knocks. "It's me," she says. "Janey."

Silence.

Finally the door opens a crack. There's Donnie's lean tan arm. He's wearing only jeans, and they're unbuttoned at the top. He stares at her.

I can see why she likes him just now. Before this moment, his so-called soulfulness seemed strict and teacherly. But now his eyes are deepened by something.

"I brought a present." She holds up the joint.

"Uh-huh," he says. "Listen . . ."

Jane talks faster. "It's yours if you want it. Or not if you don't. I brought Mary Margaret with me, and we could just hang out if that's all right."

"Jane," he says, holding up his hand, "not now. Can't."

"Oh," she says, smiling. "Sure. Maybe later tonight?"

When he nods and says, "Maybe," in a wary way, Jane says, "No problem."

The door shuts and she leans back against it. "I'm just gonna wait," she declares to no one.

Even without seeing in, I'm sure that Donnie has a girl in his room. I'm waiting for Jane, the girl with the fabulous instincts, to figure it all out.

"Maybe we should go? Home, I mean," I say. "Really, I don't mind."

Jane runs her hands through her hair, straightens her blouse, and turns to me. "Let's go get high," she says.

I follow the speeding Jane down to the kitchen, where she hops on the counter and dangles her legs. Jane lights up, smokes, and scrunches her nose. When I see Rob coming in from the backyard, I wave.

"Hey," he says. "Here you are."

"Happy summer, Rob," Jane says, hugging him.

"Are we gonna be seeing you every Friday and Saturday night?"

"Hope so," I say.

He pauses and gives us the eye. "Do your parents know you come here?"

"God. Should they?" Jane asks.

"No," Rob says emphatically. "Look, last week, we had some kid's father over here hassling us. Some high school kid."

"We're at the movies," Jane says. "Officially."

"It's cool. Just making sure," Rob says. "I've got to ask you not to tell any more of your friends about our place. 'Cause it's the last thing we need around here."

"I noticed something was going on," I say. "It's like everyone's in a funeral mood."

Rob winces. "Not the words I'd choose, but yeah."

"Oh, did someone die?" asks Jane.

Rob drops his hand on Jane's knee. "Donnie's been drafted."

Jane covers her face. "No," she whispers. "NO!"

"He got the letter yesterday afternoon, and he's got nine days to report for the physical."

"But he's a student," I tell Jane. "So he won't have to go."

"Donnie," says Jane, "is taking philosophy this summer because he wants to. He's done with school."

"So he can't get a student deferment," Rob says. "He's in trouble."

Jane hands me the joint and hops down from the counter. "I gotta talk to him."

"He's locked in his room," I tell Rob.

Jane stamps her foot. "I'll knock down the door!"

"Uh, Jane," says Rob. "I wouldn't do that if I were you."

"Why NOT?"

"Lorraine," Rob says. "His old girlfriend. She's been here since last night."

"Oh." Jane bites her lip and stares into the middle distance. I hand her the joint. When she exhales, it's as if she has shrunk a few inches.

"I don't feel anything," she says, looking down at the joint. "Does anybody have some wine?"

"Janey," says Rob softly. "A little restraint?"

"Maybe," I say, "we should go."

At first, Jane seems like she's going to fight the idea.

"Stick a pin in the map, remember?" I say. "That's all I mean." And then my heart expands as I catch sight of him. There's Mitchell, standing in the kitchen doorway. When he spots me, though, he frowns.

I wave. "Come over here!"

"I went for a walk," he says, "and then I went to the bus stop and sat. I didn't know I was coming here until the bus showed up."

I tell him about Donnie's draft letter.

"Shit," Mitch says.

"All of a sudden, it's like there's really a war," Jane says, saucer-eyed. "All of a sudden."

Mitch gives Jane a double take. "You're stoned, aren't you?"

"I'm sad," she says. "Horribly sad."

Mitch takes me aside. "Are you doing what she's doing?"

"I'm not stoned," I say. "I tried, but Jane's not sharing."

Mitch pulls on his ear and frowns. "See? This is why I'm feeling so weird. I didn't tell anyone I was going out."

"Call home, then," I say. "Say you're at the movies. Or you can go back. Though I wish you wouldn't."

He bites his lower lip and stares me down. "I don't want to leave you here."

"You didn't take me here," I say slowly. "So how can you leave me here?"

"Yeah, yeah. Still, I want you to come home. With me."

"I can't leave Jane." I search his face. "She's all wired. Can you tell me what you're so worried about?"

"Okay," he says. "I don't want you here getting high by yourself."

"Oh," I laugh, "don't worry. What can happen? No one's driving."

"I'm not talking about that," he says. He lowers his voice and looks sheepish. "You know how you get."

How I get. I chew on that for a second, then push him on the shoulder. "I only 'get' like that with you."

"I don't want anyone taking advantage of you," Mitch says. "That's all."

"You're as bad as those cops."

"What cops?" Jane asks, leaning in.

"Never mind," he says.

"What are you talking about, Mary Margaret?"

"It's none of your business," Mitch snaps.

"Mitch!" I say.

"I came here to talk to Mary Margaret," he says. "Just her."

Jane squints. "Ya know, Mitch, you not only sound like a boyfriend," she says. "You sound like a clingy, whipped boyfriend."

"You're swacked," he says, "and I don't give a shit about your opinions."

"Please, Jane," I say. "Let's go back to my house. I'm worried about you."

Jane shuts her eyes and pulls at her hair.

"Jane?" I try to touch her.

"It's not supposed to be like this. I did everything right."

I try to calm her. "Please, let's go home."

"Stop pushing me under!" she practically spits.

She shoves by and goes up to the guy who gave us the joint. She's moving her hands around and chattering, and I watch her, all mixed up about what to do, until she points a finger at me and says angrily, "Go! Go leave with your boring, safe boyfriend."

"She is out of control," Mitch says.

"She's hurting, Mitch," I say. "The guy she's hung up on has been drafted. Just don't be mean to her."

"Me? Didn't you hear what she said?"

I take Mitch out the back door into the yard. "I am trying to tell you something," I say firmly. "She's had a shock, and she's reacting. Can you please just show a little mercy?"

We're quiet, and then Mitch puts his hand on my shoulder. "You won't believe this," he says. "Or maybe you will. But I came out here because I kept thinking that maybe you were dumping me."

I turn around. "Where in the world did you get that idea?"

"I get a lot of stupid ideas, Mary Margaret." He rubs one of his eyes.

He seems so genuinely humbled and embarrassed that I immediately throw my arms around him. "If you only knew how dumb you really are."

He holds me at arm's length. I take his hand and pull him down to sit with me on the grass.

"Did I ever tell you that Elizabeth Healy and I were your secret fan club? We used to follow your every move. We thought you were a heartthrob."

"Not Elizabeth Healy," he says.

I nod yes.

"Man, I can't quite picture it."

"We always thought you were a tortured soul. But a really, really cute tortured soul."

"I never picked up on any of that," he says.

"Part of your charm," I tell him.

He eyes me doubtfully.

"You're too modest. Who knows how many more of us there were? Your admirers. We might've been legion."

"All right then, you can cut it out now," he says, already out of patience.

"Sorry. I wasn't trying to insult you."

"Maybe I'm oversensitive."

"So that's why you're always so cranky!"

"Well," he explains, "it's like this. You know my brothers. If you had brothers like mine and you were a guy, you'd have to work seriously to keep up. It's all about being tough. And I'm tough enough, I think."

"Of course," I say, although tonight Mitch is probably the least tough I've ever seen him.

"I can take a lot of crap. Only when it comes to football and basketball and beating people's heads in and all the other stuff my brothers are into, I've kind of been excused." He smiles tightly. "Because I'm the little polio boy."

"Don't call yourself that."

"Nah, it's true. I mean, I'm not getting drafted. I'm totally safe. I've always been safe."

"But it's not like you to go around saying *poor me* or asking for slack. In fact, you're sort of an island."

"But I never have to ask for extra consideration. In my family, I'm like the ugly daughter or something. I just drop back and keep out of everyone's way. Unless they want to argue with me—then I'll rip their throats out."

"I can imagine."

"Except with those cops." He tosses his head and then turns away. "I did nothing for you."

"No! You did! You handed me your shirt."

"So what? They were, like, taunting you. I should've punched one of them. My brothers would've."

"So," I say, "because you can't play football and get drafted, you believe you've become an honorary girl?"

"It's no honor."

"Hey!" I say. "Not nice. You're talking to a girl, you know."

"Well, pardon me if I don't want to be one," he says, heating up.

I readjust my tone of voice and take his hands in mine. "Now, hitting cops. What would it have proved?"

"That I can take care of you," he says.

As usual, when he's not angry, he's pure and direct and simple. I love this about him. But this statement gives me the shivers. "Oh, baby," I say. "I don't want you to take care of me." And I realize just how true this is.

Mitch looks perplexed. "Sure you do. All girls do."

I drop his hands. "No. Not me."

I can see he doesn't get it, so I go direct. "I thought you didn't want to be a boyfriend. That was our deal, Mitchell."

"Yeah, I know," he says, tense.

"Half of the reason I'm so crazy for you is because I can push you and you can push me. Neither one of us is the boss."

"How does wanting to take care of you make me THE BOSS?"

"I'm trying to explain. Like, before you, I only kissed one guy. It freaked me out because it felt like a trap. I wondered if there was something wrong with me."

"See? I won't even ask who that was," Mitch says, suddenly civilized. "How bossy is that?"

"I'm glad you're not asking, because it's not important," I say. "See, we don't do scorekeeping. Both of us give and both of us take. It's mutual. With you, it's *I'm free, you're free.*" I relax and lean against him. "We're friends."

"We're friends?" he says.

I think he sounds exasperated. "Yes! Cheer up, it's good!"
His eyes bore through me.

"Well, *aren't* you my friend? You do like me, I think."

"No, Mary Margaret," he says plainly, *"I love you."*

I wait for him to add some joke. But he just looks at me.
And it's like I've been handed this deluxe, extravagant gift,
but I can't bring myself to unwrap it.

"For you to say that," I whisper. "That is a big thing."

He pulls back and watches me. "It is," he says.

"Thank you?" I say. Oh God. And now he looks like I've
just handed back a big, weighty sack of shit.

"Anytime," he says. Without even facing me, he promptly
stands.

So I stand, too, awkwardly. Only I don't take his hand or
lean into him. I can't. "Well, I guess I gotta check on Jane,"
I tell him. I abruptly turn and head back to the house.

Okay, okay. I need to separate, need to catch my breath.
Give me a second and I'll fix everything, come up with something to say to him. I will, I will.

The kitchen is smoky and Jane isn't here. I step over the
bodies in the hallway—a favorite sitting spot for some regu-
lars. "Anyone seen Jane?" I ask. "Blond, this tall?"

"No," says Van from behind me, "but Mitch is here."

"Thanks," I say, "just saw him."

In the big parlor, where the music is dirgelike and the
drum is bubbling darkly under the bass line—one of those
songs where there doesn't seem to be a beginning, middle, or
end—I see Donnie and his old girlfriend sitting face to face,

their foreheads touching. Both clasp jelly jars of red wine and appear to be breathing in unison.

This image tells me all I need to know about their history together and how they feel about each other right now. I do know love when I see it. No way am I going to interrupt them to ask about Jane.

Has Jane seen *them*? Holy crap.

I go back to Mitch. He's not there, and neither is Jane. But Rob is there.

"Thank God! Rob, I'm looking for Jane. Have you seen her?"

"Not for the last half hour," he says. "Man, she was really worked up, don't you think?"

"I'm worried," I say.

"It's her way, I'm afraid." He points to his head.

"What do you mean, her way?"

"I'm not putting her down," he says. "I like her, too. But she has a habit of going and going until she crashes." He shrugs. "Some chicks are like that."

"Have you seen Mitch, then?"

"Just shook his hand. He headed down that way."

"He left," I say, disbelieving.

"Yeah. Guess he just came to drop by."

I sit in a corner on the floor and think about Mitchell. No one disturbs me because they probably think I'm tripping. And I am! Poor Mitch. How could I look into his naked face and see all the risk, then refuse to give anything back? What's wrong with me?

Me. Monster Girl.

Actually, no. I'm not even a monster. I'm not remarkable enough for that. I have no special talents, am average in every way—just an okay-smart, brown-haired, green-eyed, normal-type girl. But he loves me. He said it out loud.

What, exactly, does he love? I'm still *forming.* Probably the only thing that's really exceptional (revolutionary?) about me is that I'm looking for some unnameable something.

For me, *love* means "you're done." It's the word in the sentence before the final *ever after. . . .*

I look at my watch tick until midnight and recheck the bathrooms and the bedrooms and the yard. I ask Rob for a ride home and make him promise to do the same for Jane when she shows up.

"Please," I tell Rob when we get to my neighborhood, "turn off your lights and drop me off here." We're one house short of mine, and I plan on sneaking into the backyard unnoticed. "I'm sorry to be such a pain," I say.

"Anything to avoid the vengeful parent," whispers Rob. "Just remember, no more high school kids at the house, okay?"

"I promise," I say. "Bring Jane home and I'm your slave forever."

"Stay free, Mary Margaret," he says, holding up a fist. "Jane'll turn up."

I get Rob to write down the phone number to the Rainbow House on a Zig-Zag rolling paper, then close the car door softly and watch Rob drive away. After slithering through the rosebushes on the side of the house, I crawl on my hands and knees across the back patio and am peeling back the flap on the pup tent when, suddenly, I'm caught in the spotlight.

My mother.

"Nice try, young lady," she says.

I can see her silhouetted against the sliding glass door, and I can only imagine the face she's making.

"So, whose car was that, Mary Margaret? I've never seen that boy before."

"Just a friend," I say.

"And where's Jane?"

"She's coming." I hope I'm not lying.

"Inside. Now," Mother says.

Everyone else is asleep. I sit on the arm of the sofa, waiting for her to have at me. She takes the chair across from the coffee table, taps out a Pall Mall from the cardboard package. There's the flare of her match. She crosses her legs and takes a drag, all the time with eyes fixed on me.

"I'll bet," she says, "that you think I can't possibly understand you. Right?" She nods, agreeing with herself, then leans forward. "You can't imagine that I was ever your age or did things behind my mother's back because I thought I knew better."

"Did you?"

"What?"

"Know better?"

"Not nearly as much as I thought I did."

I look down at the floor.

"But I can tell you right now the invaluable thing I

learned: that there are some actions we take that will change our lives forever. Do you understand what I mean by this?"

"You're saying that once you make your bed, you have to lie in it."

"Oh, it's more than that." She waves her cigarette. "All those prayers you've said to your God since you were a little girl? They're your promise to take responsibility for your sins. So when decisions are made, terrible decisions, it's your cross to bear alone, my dear. And *you* will have to carry it."

"I intend to carry my own crosses. I always have."

"How? How have you ever had to do that?" says Mother.

I pound the sofa with my fist. "With you—the way you resent and belittle me. You're my cross!"

"Oh, I don't know," Mother says. "You might want to take that back. Think about who puts the roof over your head, the clothes on your back, and the food on your table, for starters."

"I didn't ask to be born. That's your cross to bear," I say. I watch her until she looks away. Then I ask, "When is your real anniversary, Mother?"

She jerks her head up, then eyes me steadily. "Who have you been talking to?"

"I know," I say. "You hate celebrating it on April twenty-second because it's a fake. And you hate me because I'm your lifelong cross. Along with Dad, who you also hate."

"Mary Margaret," she says. "Now you listen to me!"

"No, you listen." I stand. "You let me know it every day of my goddamn life."

"I do not," she says. "I never once said anything like that."

I fold my arms and treat her to the same look she's given me a thousand times. "You don't have to, Mom," I say. "I pay every day for being your cross. I've got your voice in my head, your temper, your frustration. . . . My fists are locked over my heart. You've done your job. But good."

She shuts her eyes, but I plunge on. "I can't help it that you married some boy you probably would've broken up with when you were eighteen."

The cigarette burns between her fingers.

"But maybe you think this is just more 'drama'?"

She keeps her face turned away.

"Who is acting like a child now? Who's not facing up to their responsibilities?" I ask. I click off the porch light from inside the living room, leave, and dive into my tent. Face-down on the old sleeping bag, I breathe in feathers. The night is a racket of crickets—so many playing at once, it sounds like the world is in an open-throated panic.

Time passes as I lie awake in dry-eyed shock. When the tent flap opens, I see it's Mother and pretend to sleep. She crawls in and is sitting on her heels, watching me. She leans over my face, and I can feel one of her teardrops splash against my temple and run into my ear. The heel of her hand is on my forehead, and I remember the way she'd check me for fever when I was a little girl. Her kiss against my neck is wet and trembling.

All my muscles tighten. "Just let me sleep, Mom. Please."

I sense her crawling back out, hear her sniffling as she heads back inside. I lie until sleep descends like a knockout punch.

Suddenly the porch light goes on yet again. I make out a shadow on the wall of my tent. Jane? On my crawl to the opening of the tent, I seem to be making the slowest progress. The space here inside seems to be lengthening like a hallway.

Keep going, says a muffled voice.

"I'm trying," I say. When I get to the opening, a woman's hands reach in to pull me out. I recognize the plain gold wedding band and the Lady Timex.

"Oh, Mother. Just please, please leave me alone."

The hands stay extended. I'm so tired. I stick out one finger halfheartedly, and the next thing I know, I'm pulled to standing outside.

My child, says the woman in the blue veil.

It's her. Mary, Mother of God. Our Lady of . . . Multnomah County?

As if on cue, I fall to my knees, but she lifts my chin so I'll look up. What a smile she has—a soft one that does not show teeth—and a brow that doesn't wrinkle and deep brown eyes, an exact replica of Elizabeth's. The logic of this strikes me as perfect. How could I have missed the resemblance all these years?

A breeze stirs the hem of her robe. I watch for a glimpse of her familiar brown sandals—the ones I've studied at nose level since I started kneeling at the communion rail. But there are no sandals, no feet. She is floating on air.

"My feet are missing," says Our Lady.

"I'm sorry," I say.

"Could you find them for me?"

"I'll look around," I tell her.

Mary regards me with a bit of disappointment. I'm expected to go forth and *find*, not just "look around." As soon as I've recognized my fault, I'm forgiven! She signifies this and blesses me with the heel of her hand on my forehead, filling me with light.

"When you go forward," she says, softly smiling, "go with open arms." She turns her palms up and poses as if for an embrace. "Now sleep," she says.

I'm grateful and teary. Not crying, but fully welled up. I bow and obey.

20

When the birds begin to chirp, it's only half light outside and there's no Jane in the tent. No Virgin Mary outside, either. I reach down into my bra and pull out the crumpled paper with Rob's number. If I go in the house and call now, I'm sure to wake somebody. Luckily, there's change in my bag enough for some phone booth calls.

It's one of those Pacific Northwest summer mornings where the clouds bear down. A little chilly in my shorts and poor-boy shirt, I lift my bike from where it lies in the front yard and make my way to the drugstore through a lumpy shortcut in a vacant lot.

My change clinks. The phone rings for a long time.

"Hullo."

"Rob?"

"It's five-thirty a.m."

"It's Mary Margaret."

A pause. "I'll get him."

"Mary Margaret?" yawns Rob. "Hey."

"She didn't come home," I tell him. "Do you know anything?"

"Yeah," says Rob. "I couldn't call you because I didn't get your number."

"Is she okay?"

"She went off with Donnie's brother, I hear. Back to Washington."

"Donnie's brother?"

"He was here last night. A tall guy, long brown hair."

I flash on the rude guy with the embroidered belt. "The guy with the rings?"

"Yeah, him."

"Why? Where?"

"What I get from Donnie is Jane heard he was packing up and going back home. So she decided to go home with Rich and wait for him there. In Centralia. It's, like, halfway between Seattle and Portland."

"Can I talk to Donnie, please?"

"Um, I don't think so," says Rob. "I'm sorry, but he's burned out on the Jane situation and he's just staying out of it."

"How nice for him," I say. "How easy."

"Yeah, well—maybe I could ask him something for you?"

"I need to know where to find her. And after he lets you know, tell him he's an asshole. From me."

When I get the Centralia address, I give Rob my home phone number. "If she calls you, let her know I'm on my way," I say.

Another phone call. This time to Greyhound. I find out how much the tickets to Centralia are, round-trip and one-way. I have all of nine dollars at home, which I cannot get without being caught.

Options:

1. Go beg Mitch, who is pissed and hurt and who would have to borrow his parents' car.

2. Go home and wait. No way.

3. Find a person who won't send out the police. Someone with a full piggy bank who trusts me well enough to trust me to pay them back. I have one idea.

It's the closest match.

I keep seeing her face framed by the Virgin's veil. Am I losing my mind?

Down back over the lumpy field, past the unchanging yards and landmarks of Thompson Avenue, I circle Elizabeth Healy's blue aluminum-sided home before stopping. It's almost six-thirty. No one will be up yet.

My breathing is almost asthmatic by the time I duck beneath her bedroom window.

Tap tap. Twice lightly with the fingernails doesn't bring Elizabeth to the window. I try it again, then finally give in to sustained tapping, hoping that holding my breath makes the whole exercise quieter.

The curtains move! I lean against the window. Her face appears. Our noses are separated by a pane of glass. She shrieks!

I cover my own mouth and shake my head NO! "It's okay!" I mouth.

Elizabeth's wavy hair lies flat on one side of her head. She's wearing her flannel nightie, the puffy one with eyelet lace that looks like something from colonial America. After a few too noisy tugs, the window squeaks along on its metal runners.

"Mary Margaret, what are you doing here?" she stage-whispers.

I realize I have no prepared statement.

"I've been sent here by Our Lady," I say.

Elizabeth turns her head slightly and gives me a sideways glance. "Huh?" she says.

"I know! Very weird, sounds like a joke. . . ."

She leans forward and peers at me. "Are you drunk?"

"What? No, no . . ."

"Look, I know that I'm *boring* and *square* and in love with church in an *uncool way*, but really, Mary Margaret. Is Jane going to pop up from behind the bushes?"

I can see her start to tug the window shut, so I stick my hand in to stop her. But Elizabeth is already putting all her weight into it, and the window slams with a bang.

I scream a backward scream where I suck in air. Elizabeth's expression mirrors mine. She jerks at the sill to free me, and my fingers fly to my mouth.

"Mmmph," I say as tears shoot out my eyes.

Elizabeth holds her hands to her throat. "I didn't mean to," she says.

I peek at my fingers, striped with white and bulging dark on the ends, and massage my knuckles. "S'okay," I say. "I guess I scared you, didn't I? You must not know what to think."

As painful as my fingers are, the slam appears to have caused Elizabeth to feel more kindly toward me. "Are you all right?" she asks.

"No," I say. "I'm not all right, and I need help."

"What kind of help?"

What the hell. "Money help."

Elizabeth doesn't even have to tell me what's running through her mind. "Oh," she says, disappointed. "For what? Marijuana?" Elizabeth folds her arms. "Word gets around."

"I've never bought marijuana in my life," I say honestly.

"Then what?" she says, her eyes positively round with alarm.

"Oh no, Elizabeth," I say, too loud, "don't even *think* I'm pregnant for a fraction of a second or I will just puke."

"Good!" she says, relieved. "Because even after everything, you know, that would make me very sad."

"Thanks. You're nice. You know that?"

"It's better than nothing," she says. "Doesn't bring the boys around, but anyhow . . ." Her smile is so sad.

"Hey, could you come out here? I don't want to wake anybody up."

She looks over both shoulders. "Wait there," she whispers.

When she comes out the front door, she's wearing her raincoat over her nightgown. It makes me secretly laugh. So Elizabeth.

We park ourselves on the painted iron bench under the front yard pine. "What's all this," Elizabeth asks, "about the Virgin Mary?"

While I tell her the dream, she concentrates on my every word. "Hmmm," she says. "That's strange. It's not like she gave you three secrets to tell the pope."

"Or to prepare for the end of the world," I say. "I know. None of the usual stuff."

"It could be just a regular dream, I guess," says Elizabeth, a little let down. Then her eyes light up. "Maybe it's a message you'll understand later. You know, if you keep your eyes and, I guess, your arms open."

"So you think it really could be her?" I ask.

"I do. I do," she says, her eyes rounding. "Just think of all the prayers you've said. I mean, on the rosary alone, there are ten Hail Marys to every Our Father. You've got a lifetime trail of prayers out to her, and she's followed them back to you." Then, very serious, she says, "Exactly what kind of trouble are you in?"

"Um," I say, "it's Jane. Jane's in trouble."

Elizabeth looks deflated. "Of course. I should have guessed," she says.

"Please listen," I say.

It's hard to get her to feel sympathy for Jane. I explain that Jane is a lot more mixed up than she appears, that she's kind of a lost sheep, that I'm the only one who can bring her back.

"Won't her parents just throw her back to House of the Good Shepherd?"

"If I can bring her home soon enough, they won't know she's gone," I say. "I know you don't like Jane. But on the other hand, you are one of the few people I know who would help out somebody you don't even like."

"Well"—she hesitates—"I don't have the whole thirty-five dollars." I beg her for what she's got and promise to pay back every penny.

"You do know me," I tell her. "I'm still basically dependable and responsible, no matter how hard I've tried to change."

"Oh, I trust you, Mary Margaret," she says. She bites her thumbnail. "I just never, ever thought I'd help you hitchhike out of state." She makes a face. "Wait here. I'll get the money."

It's a little past seven. I watch Elizabeth return with a cylinder of folded bills, mostly ones, bundled with a rubber band. There's just enough for two one-way tickets back from Centralia. She places the wad in my hand.

"Thank you," I say. "And also . . . I just want you to know how much I've been thinking about David. You know, what you said about being good for him?"

"It might not make sense to you," says Elizabeth. "But I know that if I was God and I wanted to punish me, the worst punishment I can think of would be to lose my brother."

"Oh, Elizabeth. I don't think the stupid war is about punishing you. If the world ran on whether or not Elizabeth Healy was a good person, we'd be living in a damn paradise."

She sort of smiles. "Well, stupid or not," says Elizabeth, "David's over there. America's got to stay till we've won. I know that, believe me. My father tells me all the time."

"Why shouldn't America quit? Why can't we ever turn around and try something different?" I ask. "See, this is something I've been thinking about a lot lately. Whether it's war or getting married or going to church or whatever. Why do we keep doing the same things?"

"You mean, why can't EVERYTHING change?"

"Okay, yes. Why not?"

"Because that's the way things have always been?" Elizabeth shrugs.

"But nothing's always been. Think about it!"

Elizabeth thinks. "Here's a reason," she offers. "People in the olden days figured things out little by little. And now we live by their wisdom."

Elizabeth speaks so simply. Her legs are crossed at the ankles, her hands in her lap. I'm reminded of a photograph of my mother at eighteen, sitting on a wooden bench with a bough of ripe apples looming over her head.

"No," I say. "I can't believe it. They can't have figured everything out perfectly hundreds of years ago and now we just have nothing left to . . . to make better. Where's, like, the sense in that?"

"You're asking me?"

"I don't want to do things just because other people *say* I should."

"But there's always hell, Mary Margaret. Remember hell?" Elizabeth says this gently, as if she has my best interests at heart.

This is what it's like to be part of Elizabeth's world. It's my world, too, somewhat. "You can't argue with hell," I concur.

"At least that's one thing we still agree on."

"No. I mean it's a thing you can't reason with. I hate feeling like every time I start thinking, I'm just marching down the hallway to a locked door."

"Or hitchhiking up a busy freeway to who knows where," Elizabeth says.

"God, Elizabeth," I say. "I almost forgot. I'm really going to hitchhike to Centralia."

For someone who would never hitchhike herself, Elizabeth is full of practical ideas for my trip. Because it's cloudy and getting chilly, she gives me her coat off her back and reattaches the detachable hood. She decides I'll need a destination sign to hold up, so she gives me the flap from a cardboard box and a black crayon. Finally, she hands me little chunks of Tillamook cheese in wax paper for the road. And napkins!

"You can leave your bike here," she says, "and take a city bus as far as downtown. Then get a transfer to take you up toward Jantzen Beach. Then you need to get over the bridge into Washington and onto I-5 north."

With Elizabeth doing the planning, I feel more confident, well organized. "You have been so good to me. I can't thank you enough."

"For old times' sake," she says. Then, tearing up, she adds, "No hard feelings."

"None," I say. And I know now she's talking about Mitch.

We hug, she promises prayers for my safety—"and, okay, Jane's, too"—and she actually blows me a kiss, proudly, as if I'm off to my first day of kindergarten. Which I was once, walking hand in hand with her.

21

My big challenge on the bus is to contain my terror. The streets are beginning to spatter with rain. Will there be a downpour? Do I hold up the sign *and* stick out my thumb? What will I do if a creepy man stops? Can I scrawl WOMEN ONLY on my hitchhiking sign? Do women ever actually pick up hitchhikers?

But by the time I transfer to the Jantzen Beach bus—the last warm, safe miles with a certified uncrazy driver at the wheel—I'm frozen with misgivings. I can see down into the police car in the lane beside us and wonder if I'll get picked off the highway before I can even get started. Do I secretly want that?

The last stop is at the amusement park with the famous wooden roller coaster that tempts families from the freeway. How I wish I could take my wad of dollar bills and spend a day on the bumper cars. Instead, I take a trek away from the park to the semicircular freeway entrance where enormous lumber trucks and pickups kick up gravel and rainwater.

I've never stood at a freeway entrance before. It's thunderous. My cardboard sign I grip in my teeth while I pull my hood (good old Elizabeth!) down over my eyebrows. A powerful mix of embarrassment and fear makes my knees knock whenever I hold up the sign.

The whoosh of the bigger cars blows me back. HELLO! I'M DEFENSELESS! DON'T HURT ME! is what my sign should say.

Just when the roar and swish of traffic has begun to hypnotize me, a red Ford Ranchero signals and pulls ahead of me on the shoulder. It's a man; that much I can make out.

Hugging the damp sign to my chest, I run up to his window. It's a guy with black-plastic-and-wire-rimmed glasses and a tight-to-the-head barbershop haircut. Okay, he's kind of old—old enough for me to have a chance in a fight, if I have to.

He waves me in, and I hop in the passenger's seat.

"Seat belt," he says. He's grumpy, I think. As soon as I'm buckled up, he tears out onto the road. He doesn't drive like an old guy.

"You want to tell me what you're doing out here?" he says. "On a day like this?"

His scolding makes me scrunch down in my seat. "Going to Centralia," I say.

"Your name," he states.

"Mary . . . Jane," I say.

"How old are you? All of sixteen, I should think."

I stare out the window, hoping he'll stop talking. We are

approaching the bridge that takes us across the Columbia River to the state of Washington.

"Look here," he says. "You know how much trouble I could get in, transporting a minor across state lines?"

"No."

"Federal offense," he continues. "I must be out of my cotton-pickin' mind."

"Well, thank you, anyway," I say. "For picking me up." I try to smile like a well-brought-up granddaughter.

"You read the papers, Mary Jane?" he asks.

"Sometimes," I say.

"Carry identification?"

"What?"

"Do you or don't you have with you a driver's license or other form of identification?"

He overpronounces everything. I try to guess the response that will calm him down. "Got a library card," I say.

"Got a library card," he mutters to himself. "Fat lot of good that'll do."

We hit the corrugated steel floor of the bridge, and a tuba-like groan threatens to drown out the old man's grousing.

"Hitchhikers' bodies have been found under three bridges in the next two counties!" he shouts. "An extraordinarily foolhardy enterprise, young lady! I tell you this not just as a father, but as an ordained minister!"

We finally exit the bridge, and his voice retains full volume.

"You are danged lucky!" he booms. "I'm doing for you what I'd have done for my daughter! Or the parents of that poor college girl strangled up in Castle Rock!"

Since there is no correct facial expression I can think of, I concentrate on the man's Adam's apple, rising and falling behind his string tie secured with a hunk of agate.

"Broken neck," he says.

Oh my Lord, my Lord. What have I gotten myself into? My skin is prickling with alarm. Every little hair is standing up in its follicle. I check the traffic ahead, trying to calculate at what speed I can fling open the car door, leap, and still survive. I wonder why Elizabeth didn't include a kitchen knife with my hitchhiking supplies.

"Are you listening to what I'm telling you?" he asks.

"Yes, sir," I say. "Absolutely."

For the next half hour, he talks about the world *going to hell in a handbasket*—which has something to do with boys growing their hair out like girls and girls going wild, which somehow always brings us back to one grisly crime or maiming incident after another.

"So," he continues, "as I was saying, that's one kid who's gonna go his whole life with no thumbs. And *he's* a lucky one!"

And then I hear the *click click* of the turn signal. The old man is turning off the freeway.

"Where are we going?" Tensing, I take a mental inventory of all my available means of defense. *Fingernails and teeth and knees,* I tell myself.

"Gonna fill up here," he says.

I check his gas gauge. It's still over a quarter full.

We roll onto a strip of asphalt that's lined with a mom-and-pop grocery, a tire store, a coffee shop, and, finally, a gas station. I know I'm gonna bolt. But where to?

The attendant comes out, and as he starts wiping the windows, I see an old, dusty Plymouth pull up at the other pump. The backseat is piled with clothing and books, and the people up front look friendly and young, maybe still in their twenties. The man has hair my old guy wouldn't approve of. The woman stands and stretches, pushes her round sunglasses on the top of her head, and walks toward the pop machine.

"Oh my gosh!" I say.

"What's wrong now?" says the old man, as if I'd been complaining the entire trip.

"Nothing!" I chirp. "That's Leslie! My friend! Right there! Leslie! Unbelievable! She was who I was going to see!"

I skip on over past the Plymouth until I'm standing with the woman. "Help me," I say, locking my jaws into a grin. "Pretend you know me. I've got to get away from this guy. . . ."

The lady lunges forward and gives me a bear hug. "That man in the red car?" she whispers.

"I'm hitching and he scares me," I say.

She takes my hand and leads me over to my ride. "Hello!" she says cheerfully. "How nice of you to give a ride to my friend. I see you've taken good care of her."

"Who are you?"

That's none of your business, I think, but I humor him by reminding him (and her) that it's Leslie Gore, my math teacher from my old high school.

"Anyway," says Leslie, "thanks for keeping her safe. We'll take it from here."

"While you're teaching her," says the old man, "you might include a lesson on the stupidity of riding with strangers."

"Will do. Thanks again!" she says, draping her arm around my shoulders. She guides me to her car.

"Is he gone?" I ask.

"Leaving right now," she says. "Who was he?"

"Never even got his name," I say.

She laughs. "I'm Holly, by the way. And that guy there in the car? That's my husband, Allen."

"I'm Mary Margaret," I tell her, "and you were wonderful."

"It was nothing," Holly says. "Where are you going now?"

Immediately my stomach curdles as I think about going back on the freeway. "I have to get to Centralia," I say, "to see my friend. She needs me, and I don't drive, and I don't have enough money for the bus."

"Allen and I are headed to Seattle. You want to ride with us?"

I clasp my hands under my chin to show my undying gratitude. "Yes, please! Thank you!"

"C'mon," Holly says. "I'll introduce you."

Both Holly and Allen are headed to the University of Washington, where Holly is teaching a class about folktales. "They teach that in college?" I ask. "Doesn't sound like any class I've ever heard of."

They laugh at that. "You sound exactly like Holly's mother," Allen says.

Oops.

Allen asks if I've considered going to college at UW. I tell him I've never even considered going to any college.

"Don't rule it out," Holly says. "You don't need a ton of money. You can get loans."

"No one in my family has ever gone," I say.

"Definitely not a requirement," says Holly.

"Listen to Holly," says Allen, in a mock-parent kind of tone.

They're both so cute, I can't get over it. I picture them together in some ramshackle little house loaded with books and coffee cups filled with pencils and maybe a cat.

"Seriously, Mary Margaret," Holly says, "what do you want to do with your life?"

"Nothing," I say.

"Oh, you must have some ideas!" Holly says. "Just look at you, thumbing by yourself through the big wide world. You've got guts, obviously."

No one has ever asked me the "big picture" question. To quote Donnie (for once), what does that say about me?

"I don't know exactly what I am interested in or what I want to do," I say. "All I can tell you is something's happened to me in the last four months. I've broken the law. Over and over! I've never done that before."

"Do you wish you hadn't?" Holly asks.

"Not really," I say. "Before, when I was good, I was really just gutter-balling my way to some predestined dead ending."

Holly rests her elbows on the backrest. "You're kind of young to be having any kind of ending, don't you think?"

I sit and think about this. *Yes. Exactly.*

The hour flies by, and soon the Centralia exit sign appears. I'm grateful that both of them insist on helping me find the house where Jane is staying.

Allen stops and asks a mom pushing a stroller for directions. The neighborhood we end up in is so dark and overhung with Douglas fir that moss grows on the sides of the houses. Someone keeps turkeys behind a wire fence. A miniature tractor is parked in another front yard. It's hard to picture Donnie coming from a place like this.

At two-thirty in the afternoon, we come to a stop in front of a little house with a cement porch.

"Do you want us to wait?" Holly asks.

"Would you mind?" Before I can lose my nerve, I run to the porch and knock. A woman with gray hair and blue jeans answers the door.

"Yes?" she says gruffly. She's looking around at my feet.

"Hi," I say. "I'm a friend of Donnie's. . . ."

"Ah. Okay." She relaxes. "I thought you were selling something."

"No. Actually, I'm looking for Rich. Is he here?"

"Yeah. He's out back, soldering," she says. "Through the gate."

What's soldering? I wave to Holly and Allen to let them know I've found Rich. When I get to the backyard, I see him leaning over a workbench, his hair tied back in a bandanna. I think he's making jewelry. He drops his pliers when I come near. "What do you want?" he asks.

"I'm looking for Jane Stephens," I say. "I'm a friend of hers and Donnie's. Mary Margaret? We met at Rob's last night."

"Poor Donnie."

I hold my arms down at my sides, though I'd really like to smack him.

"If you're looking for a place to stay," he says, wiping his hands on an old rag, "I can't help you."

"I just want Jane."

"She's in there," he says. At the back of the acre, I can see a two-tone camper on the back of a well-worn truck. "Just take her off my hands, will you?"

"I'm here to do just that," I say.

"She's nuts, you know," he says, standing. "Last night, she talked nonstop about all kinds of shit, and now I can't wake her up. She fed me a line about having family in Centralia and I wasn't in my right mind, so here we are. I'm going to hate myself for asking, but how old is she?"

"Sixteen," I say.

Rich's eyes roll back in his head. "Worse than I thought," he says.

He opens the creaky camper door and directs me inside. I see a lump on the mattress, covered completely with a blanket. Light is flooding in, but the sleeper doesn't move. As I come closer, I can make out a length of Jane's pretty hair hanging over the edge of the bed.

"Jane?"

I am pierced with grief at the sight of her. Kneeling, I peel back the blanket from her head and shoulders. Her lips are pulled down into a scowl, and she has a scratch on her cheek. I put my hand on her forehead, just as my mother did to me.

"Jane, honey," I say. "Can you hear me?"

Jane takes in a breath and shrugs me off. I grab her shoulder firmly and shake. "Jane Stephens, wake up!"

Scooting next to her on the mattress, I lift her from behind the neck into a sitting position. Her eyes fly open, and she seems blankly frightened, like a startled sleepwalker.

I take her hand. "Jane, it's me. Mary Margaret. Are you all right?"

There's a twitch of recognition, and then her eyes spill over. She falls on me, hugging me hard. "Mary Margaret. Mary Margaret."

"I've come to take you home," I say, rubbing her back. She sobs for a minute, and I don't interrupt. When she calms, I look around the camper for her things.

"I got your bag," I say, "but where are your shoes?"

"Lost," Jane says.

"Anything else?"

She digs around in the covers and grabs a wrinkled jacket.

"We're good, then." I force a smile, and she almost smiles back. "C'mon, I'll help you out."

Jane is shaky when I help her down to the grass. The jacket I place on her shoulders immediately falls off when she doubles over. First she chokes, then pukes all over the truck's bumper.

"Dear God," she says.

Thank you, Elizabeth. There's a napkin in my bag. "Don't worry about it," I say, wiping her lips. "Although I'd like to get out of here before that Rich has something to say about this."

Amazingly, Holly and Allen are still parked in front of

the house. When Holly sees how bad off Jane is, limping and leaning onto me for support, she bolts from the car and takes Jane's other arm.

We make room for her in the crowded backseat with all the odds and ends from Holly and Allen's move. Holly has Allen go over to the garden and wet a washrag with a hose. I take it, fold it in thirds, and place it on Jane's forehead. We pull away and head to the Greyhound station.

"Too much to drink last night?" Holly asks.

"Too much everything," says Jane. She closes her eyes and reaches over to my lap for my hand.

"Are you fit to travel?" asks Holly, concerned.

"I'll make it," says Jane. "I have a good nurse."

Holly writes her address and phone number for me when we get to the depot. "Let me know you got home all right."

Jane, a little less wobbly now, can walk without my support. She gives the two a salute before we leave. "How do you know them?" she asks me.

"From hitching," I say.

"All the way from Portland?"

"All the way."

"You're unbelievable," she says. "For me?"

"For both of us."

By the time we're inside, Jane's ready to collapse into one of the orange plastic seats.

"I'll get our tickets," I tell her. "We'll have quite a wait. The next bus doesn't leave till six-thirty."

"Let's sit," Jane says. She stretches her bare legs out before her and reaches over for her bag, which she hugs to herself like a stuffed animal.

"Jane," I say, "do you know why you did this?"

She puts her hands to her cheeks and closes her eyes. "Honestly? Because someone said Donnie was moving his stuff back home. And I found out about that girl up in his room. And so I thought if I went to Centralia, I could get him alone and win him back." She gives in to a little shudder, as if she realizes how pathetic she sounds. Then she says, "And if I couldn't get him back, at least he'd know I'd been with his brother."

"I don't know what to say."

"I'm disgusting," she says.

"Not disgusting," I say.

"And reckless and promiscuous," she says darkly. "Someday soon, I'll be walking through traffic in my underwear."

"That's possible," I say, studying Jane. The resemblance to Yvette is kind of startling.

"Although about what happened last night, I'm afraid I can't remember it all." She pulls her knees up to her chest. "Did Donnie . . . say anything to you?"

"Donnie," I say, "is a selfish ass."

"But did he say anything?"

"Jane, he does not care about you."

She looks shaken.

I keep going. "I tried. Rob said Donnie was wiping you from his memory banks. You were too inconvenient for him."

"He said that," she says quietly.

"As for that girl up in his room, everyone says he's in love with her."

"I get it," Jane says. "Okay? Enough."

I go to the ticket booth and give her a minute to let it all sink in. When I return, she still has her head on her knees.

"Jane," I say, tapping her on the shoulder, "the lady who sold me the ticket says you can't ride the bus with bare feet."

Jane lifts her head and drops her jaw, looking a hundred years old. "What are we going to do?"

I pull off my tennis shoes and hand her my socks. "These will work," I say. Then I give her the Greyhound envelope with the one-way ticket. "A good ticket," I say. "Unlike some boys we know."

"Thank you," Jane says, turning the envelope over in her hands. "Sincerely. It doesn't show, but I am most humbly grateful."

"You're most humbly welcome. And I hope you know he doesn't deserve you, anyway," I say.

"To be fair," Jane says, "it's not him. It's all me, you know."

"What do you mean?"

"I want things, and then I plot for them." Jane moves her hands up and down like weights on a scale. "It's like desire and scheme, desire and scheme. Go, go, go."

"You're . . . passionate," I say.

"Except at first, it feels like I'm the one making everything happen, and then when I get going fast, I feel like something is pushing me." She gives me a pleading look. "Does this ever happen to you?"

"Not like it does with you."

"And I let people down," she says. "You're the first person, the first, not to get rid of me."

"That's what girlfriends do," I say.

"Mary Margaret," she says, whispering, "I've never had a girlfriend."

"Believe me. When you're in trouble," I say, "girlfriends are *always* the best tickets."

"I see that now, I really do," says Jane. "But . . ."

"What?" I say.

"But can we still have boys on the side?" Jane asks.

"Well, I still want mine," I tell her. "But you, maybe you should come up with a plan B. Fresh start, nice guy?"

"Oh, Mary Margaret," Jane says, "if you only knew how *incredibly* tired I am."

I pat my shoulder, showing her where to lay her head. Soon I hear a soft snore.

As I watch Jane sleep, her face pale as a pearl, I do my own scheming. We'll get our stories straight, fend off our parents, beg a second chance. We'll swear off the Rainbow House and getting stoned and Jane will get back all her shiny genius and sense of adventure. Maybe we'll even do some *real* traveling. Because as scary as today was, I'm amazed at how much the world can expand in one afternoon.

"There's still more summer left . . . ," I say out loud.

22

We get close to Portland at eleven o'clock, and Jane and I agree that if no one's awake at home, we'll just go straight to bed. No talking about what went on or where we've been until we're asked. Then we'll just say we've been bumming around downtown.

"Make sure to blame everything on me," I tell her. "I got in an argument with my mother, I didn't want to come home, you didn't want to leave me. . . ."

"That might work," Jane says.

"Better comb your hair," I say. "And give your face a splash."

"Can I tell her you borrowed my shoes?" Jane asks. I say, "Yes, anything."

She cleans up nicely at the Greyhound station. When the city bus reaches home, she's able to fake wide awake and ready.

"Thank you, thank you, Mary Margaret," she says.

"You're welcome," I say.

"How can I repay you?"

There is one way. "Promise me that you'll forget about Donnie. Scrub your brain with Palmolive if you have to."

"I promise," she says. "Absolutely."

We hug. "Goodbye!" I call after her.

"Oh, sweetie," she says. "Let's just say au revoir!"

It's 11:45 p.m., and all the lights are on at my house. My courage shrinks when I open the door and see Mother and Dad at the dinette.

They are drinking coffee. The ashtray is overwhelming.

Paula, in her pink pajamas, slides down the hall and peeks around the corner.

"Back to bed!" says my dad.

"I just wanted to see if that was her," says Paula.

"Bed!" my father repeats.

"I'll talk to you tomorrow, Paula."

Mother sits with her arms folded.

"Nice to see you, Mary Margaret," Dad says.

"I've been downtown," I say.

"We called the Dunns first," my dad says. "Mitch said he hadn't seen you. No information at all from him. He seems worried. He wants us to call when we find you."

"I got in a fight with Mom," I say. "And I just took off—"

"Then, as soon as we could, we got hold of the Stephenses," continues my father, talking right over me. "Mr. Stephens came over and we had a visit."

"Aren't you going to let me explain?" I ask.

"No. I'm not!" Dad barks. I shut up.

Mom is still hanging back. I've never seen my dad this mad and in charge.

"We didn't know about Jane," Dad says. "Her history of . . . you know. Her father told us everything. He was very apologetic. They seem to think she's been a bad influence on you."

"No, Dad. It's not Jane's fault."

Mother finally speaks. "Apparently Mrs. Stephens knows this new boy . . . Rob, is it? Your father and Mr. Stephens went over there looking for you."

"You went to Rob's? Dad!"

"I did."

"Jane and Rob are just friends," I say. "Didn't he tell you that?"

"That's what he claims," Dad says. "But he also said you and she come over at times to that house full of hippies and drifters and God knows what else. . . ."

I put my hands over my face. "They're going to hate me. They are going to hate me. . . ."

"They know that if you are ever seen over there again, they are to send you home," says my father. "Or else."

I open my mouth.

"On top of that, you're not leaving this house for three weeks."

"Let me explain. Please . . ."

"*And* your friendship with that girl is officially over."

"No!" I stamp down hard and yell. "That's not fair!"

"And if you don't shut your mouth and go to your room right now," he says grimly, "I'm afraid I can't be responsible for what I'll do."

Who *is* this man?

"I can't *believe* you won't let me see Jane!" I say.

Now my father stands and pushes back his chair. I jump up and stagger to the bathroom, lock the door, sit on the toilet, and bury my face in a towel, my shoulders shaking. Would he have hit me?

When I get myself together, I stand and look at my bleary face in the mirror. I wonder how Mother got Dad to act like this.

I need sleep.

I go to my room, kick off my shoes, and make my way to my bed in the dark. Paula's crying, and my dad is talking to my mother in a low voice. "She's growing up so fast, and I didn't even notice," he says.

Mother talks back soothingly. I hope Paula hears that, at least. Mom hasn't spoken that way to my father—to any of us—in a long time.

I'm awakened by banging garbage cans. Paula and Katie are already up. The sunlight cuts across the west wall of my bedroom, spotlighting the worn wallpaper.

Mother opens the door and waits. I won't look at her, so she makes her way over and sits on my bed.

"Your father's gone," she says. "Left for work."

"What do you want?" I ask.

"I know you don't think we're doing this out of love. But we are."

"Well, thank you very much," I say darkly.

"Your dad just woke up and smelled the coffee. Especially after he saw that hippie house. He says that this Rob has hair longer than yours. He had a fit when he saw that."

"So, this is all about *Rob's hair?*"

"Of course not. You've always been his good oldest girl . . . and he was a teenager once. He won't have you compromised."

Compromised. What a stupid word.

"But here's what we've worked out," she continues. "Later, if Mitchell wants to come over, you can have him visit you here."

I stare at the ceiling.

"Because at least he's a boy your own age from the parish. And now we know he's a straight arrow, from what we can gather. . . ."

Who have they been talking to?

"And we have to expect you'll want to go out with boys. But in the proper way, of course."

"Okay, I'll go along. But then, I don't have a choice, do I?" I say softly.

Mother puts her hands in her lap. "Yes. That's what I'm saying." She nods. "And if you want a fight, you're going to have to have it with your father." She stands, and on her way out, she shuts the door gently.

After half an hour of lying on my back, I realize that three more weeks is going to seem like an eternity. I sit up, hug my pillow, and wonder what Jane is doing now. Will she lie around on her bed all morning? No, I'm sure she won't.

The thing is to keep going forward, to use this restlessness that's driving me crazy and look for any opportunity to survive this mess.

Where to start, though? I don't have phone privileges. I'll have to call Elizabeth when no one's looking and let her know I'm okay. One thing is sure, I'll get nowhere with my parents by being openly defiant. So I decide on a new motto: Outward Cooperation, Inward Resistance. I jump up and follow my mother's voice to the kitchen.

"I'm going to take off my wallpaper," I say. "Paint my room and everything."

"That's an awful big job, Mary Margaret," Mother says.

"I've got three whole weeks," I say.

She actually lets me pick out the color and helps me gather rollers, brushes, and two gallons of robin's egg blue latex.

The work is mind-numbing. But I don't care. I man the ancient wallpaper steamer and listen to my transistor radio while imagining what Jane might be up to. Will she be at mass on Sunday? Will she sneak out and throw a pebble at my window—or make me a cake with a file in it?

I have to sit down whenever the Supremes sing, "Love is here and oh, my darlin', now you're gone." The song plays every couple of hours, and though I'm tempted to turn it off, the pictures it brings up are too tender and precious. Heartache is a different kind of pain, isn't it? It's almost addictive. So I decide to completely give myself over to these two-minute, thirty-seven-second crack-ups, then stand, wipe my cheeks, and pick up the paintbrush again.

My dad peeks in every once in a while, and I can tell it satisfies him, seeing me all covered in limp wallpaper and Spackle. My mother doesn't complain about us girls sleeping all over, in the living room, out in the tent.

I keep my cool, waiting until I'm into my fifth day on the job, sanding cracked windowsills, when my mother goes out to the grocery store. She's gone up the street before I pick up the receiver and dial.

The Stephenses' phone rings. And rings and rings. I hang up, pour myself some ice tea, and dial again. I'm starting to get a sick feeling. Could they have sent Jane off somewhere? The doorbell dings. I slam down the phone and scoot across the room.

"Mary Margaret!" Katie calls. "It's for yoooouu!"

My heart warms. I knew she'd come through! My bare feet slip on the linoleum as I barrel my way to the door.

"Hey."

It's Mitch, looking especially darling. I smooth my hair back and pull my T-shirt straight. "I'm painting," I say.

"Is it okay if I'm here?" he asks.

"Very okay." At least I think so.

"Well," he says. "Am I gonna come in?"

"I'm under house arrest," I say. "Let's go out back."

As Mitch follows me through the side yard, he doesn't grab my hand. When we sit in old collapsing lawn chairs, he pulls his close until we're facing knee to knee. He still doesn't touch me.

"Did your dad tell you I called?" he asks.

"No," I say. "No one told me anything."

"I called the day after you got back, just to check in."

"I'm okay."

"Are you? I just want to tell you that I didn't tell your folks anything. I wouldn't do that."

"I know," I say.

"But still," Mitch says, "I left, then you turn up missing. . . . It was hard to know what to do."

"You did fine." I'm so glad to see his face, I want to sit and gaze at it. He shifts in his chair uncomfortably. There's too much unsaid stuff between us. Then I hear a bump against the sliding glass door.

"We've got spies," Mitch says. "That lump in the curtains looks like your sisters."

"I see you guys!" I holler.

The curtain empties, and we hear Katie and Paula giggle through the glass.

"Do you see what I go through around here?" I wait until I think the coast is clear, then lean forward. "So, Mitch," I whisper, "have you heard anything about Jane?"

"Nah," he says. "Why would I?"

"I don't know. Maybe you've seen her around? I'm not allowed to talk to her, but I just snuck a call and no one's there. What if they sent her away again?"

"From what I can tell from your dad," Mitch says, "everyone thinks Jane's mixed up with Rob. How's that? I just kept out of it."

"I'm scared," I say. "Wouldn't you think she'd at least try to get through to me by now?"

He sighs and folds his arms. "Don't ask me."

"Do you think that maybe you could try to get a note to her?"

Mitch looks wary.

"Please?"

"I don't want to," he says slowly. "But I will. If it's that important to you."

"It is," I say. "And I'll never forget it." I grab Mitch's wrist and look at his watch. "Damn!" I say. "My mom'll be right back."

I run to the kitchen and yank an old page from the daily calendar. On the back I write:

Grounded 3 weeks otherwise surviving. Please write back or give Mitch msg. I'm WORRIED sick about you!!
Let's meet—or call me Fridays, 10 a.m. Mom will be gone for Katie's swim lesson.
Keep the faith, sweetie! Peace, Mary M.

Pressing the note into Mitch's hand, I lean forward and kiss his face. He touches that place on his cheek. "You still like me, don't you?" he says.

His *I love you* is now obviously on both our minds. "I do like you," I say. "As much as you like me. I'm sure of it."

"Ah," he says. "We'll just have to decide what to call it, right?"

"Right."

We kiss again, for real this time.

"I'll be back," Mitch says, "with whatever I can scrape together. Is there a time I should call?"

"You can just come by," I say. "I don't know how you did it, but you won my mother over."

"Didn't do a thing." He frowns. "I'm just guessing that now your parents figure you could do a lot worse."

23

Friday passes and still no call. The next time Mitch drops by, it's only to tell me that he can't find Jane. But my mom's radar is activated, and she's soon butting in.

"Have you come to help paint?" she asks, trying to sound friendly, but I can see the suspicion peeking through.

"Sure," he says.

"Really?" I say.

"Of course," he says, like the idea was his own.

With the curtains stripped and the light streaming in and all our furniture heaped in the middle and covered with a tarp, our bedroom looks like a warehouse.

"Take it in while you can," I tell him. "This is probably the only time my mother will allow you and me together in this room."

"We'll always have the golf course, Mary Margaret," he says.

"Do you ever wonder . . . like, what's next?"

"Meaning?"

"How will this all work next year? How are my parents going to stuff me back into my old life? Isn't that delusional?"

"That's their job," Mitch says. "Probably especially with a girl."

"But it won't work," I say, lowering my voice. "Listen, I know you don't like Jane, but if there's one thing she's taught me, it's that there's always another way out. We have a friendship that can't just be broken because our parents say so."

"If she's still around," Mitch says.

"We'll find a way," I say. "If I don't figure something out, she will for sure." I dip a roller into the bright blue paint. "In the meantime," I say, "we got a whole lot of fumes to inhale."

"Right," says Mitch, breathing in. "Who needs the Rainbow House when you can get high *and* a headache right here at home?"

I laugh. "You're being so nice to me, you know that? After everything . . . You're not just any guy, Mitchell Dunn."

He takes a paintbrush, dips it in blue. I KNOW, he scrawls on the bare wall. And he keeps on painting.

On my last Friday grounded, I'm trying not to expect a call from Jane. It's been so long, I've just assumed that she's been carted off to relatives or whisked away on some "vacation" by her freaked-out parents. But when the phone rings, precisely at ten, I let out a pent-up howl. It's her. I just know it's her.

Kevin gets to the phone first. "It's a girl," he says to me.

I think I might start crying. I grab the receiver. "Hello?" I say softly.

"Sweetie!"

"Oh, Jane." Then I choke up. "I've been crazy worried."

"I know. Mother and I ran into Mitch this morning," Jane says. "At the car wash!"

"Where have you been these past three weeks?"

"Since I've seen you last," she says, "I've been around the world. I mean, I've lived a whole other life. Mary Margaret, it has been extraordinary."

I feel a twinge of disappointment. "I've just been grounded," I say. "And missing you."

"That is so sweet," she says.

I grit my teeth. "Jane, would you please tell me what the hell you're going on about?"

"Oh," she says, "you sound mad. I really need your complete and total understanding."

"You got it," I say. "Tell me."

"Okay, here it is. Something has unfolded for me. My fate has become clear, you know? I have everything, everything I ever wanted."

I'm silent, waiting.

"I am getting married next week. To Donnie."

There's a quiet roar in my head. "Excuse me?" I say.

"It's unbelievable how it's worked out." She pauses. "Mary Margaret, I'm going to have a baby."

I don't believe it.

"I'm stunned" is all I can say. "Stunned."

"So was I, at first. Mom and Avery took me to the beach. While I was there, I missed my period. I was delirious. So scared. But then I decided to *play* it. I told my mom."

"What did she do?"

"I don't think she believed me. She made calls and found a doctor that does this new early pregnancy test. I was right, of course. Then she kept me in the cabin for days, pleading, pleading. You know, both Avery and Mom wanted me to get rid of it. But they can't do that. By law."

Jane starts gushing about Donnie needing to avoid the draft, her parents being totally sick of her. Sick enough to sign off on her wedding.

"Now Mom is angry at me, of course. She can hardly stand to speak to me. But she's given up. And that's the important thing."

"Jane, you need more time," I say firmly. "You need to think this over."

"I've already thought about everything. See, now my whole life makes sense. Because if I hadn't tried to run off before with Roger, my parents never would've given in to this marriage. So I've paved the way for this. It's dharma."

"What about his girlfriend?"

"She's not pregnant," Jane says simply.

"You do realize you are going to have a little baby to take care of," I remind her. "A whole new person, for ever and ever."

"I know," Jane says. "I'm not scared about that particularly. Look at you. You're practically a mother yourself, with all the stuff you do at home. Even little Paula takes care of the baby. I figure if you girls can do it, I can."

"It's not really the same, Jane. This baby will be all your responsibility. And Donnie," I say, "how does he feel about this?"

"Donnie," says Jane, "sees it as an opportunity. A form of grace is what I call it."

I am to be at city hall on Saturday at eleven. I am the maid of honor.

"What happened to . . . all the things we talked about on the way home? I can't put this together in my mind," I say.

"It is mind-altering, isn't it?" Jane says happily. "All those old barriers have just been blown away."

"Jane, listen. . . ."

"Can't, sweetie, gotta go get a dress. Please be there on the most important day of my life?"

When Jane hangs up, I stand there listening to the dial tone.

Dazed, I go back to my room. Boxes of my childhood junk are there waiting to go up on my newly painted shelves. I sink down on the bed.

My God, I'm exhausted. I feel like I've taken a pill. I fall sideways, tuck in my knees, close my eyes, and let the world disappear.

"Mary Margaret," Katie says.

I crack open an eye and see her standing by my bed in her wet braids.

"Hey, Katie," I say.

"Why are you asleep?"

I yawn. "Just got tired."

"Do you have the measles?"

"No. I got the measles when I was your age. You can't get them twice."

Katie wrinkles her forehead. "Oh," she says doubtfully.

I roll off the bed and go to the bathroom. It isn't until I reach for the toilet paper that I see the inside of my arm—which is completely covered with spots.

I press my skin with my finger. The dots are raised, and they itch. I pull up my T-shirt. My stomach is covered. Only my face seems to have escaped the spotting.

"Mom!" I yell, pulling up my shorts. "*Mooom!*"

She's outside with Kevin, bringing in groceries from the station wagon. I thrust out my arms. "What's wrong with me?"

The question hangs in the air, loaded with all of my feelings. Mother looks at me, alarmed. My skin is now crawling, like it's trying to drive me out. The next sound out of me is a big sob. I'm having a goddamn nervous breakdown in my stupid driveway.

I'm still crying while Mother has me in the bathroom, gently dotting me with calamine. She keeps telling me to please calm down, that I have a simple case of hives. That they'll be gone in hours. She knows this because my father gets them.

"I don't remember Dad breaking out like this," I say.

"When he was young, he did," Mother says. "In fact, if you want to know . . ." Mother takes a breath and looks at me frankly.

218

"What?"

"He broke out with them on our wedding day." She shrugs, then adds coolly, "Gee, I wonder why?"

"Jane's getting married," I say.

Mother actually drops the calamine bottle. We both stare as it leaks pinkly out onto the bathroom floor.

I pick up the bottle, and calamine runs down my arm. "I can't believe I told you that."

"To that Rob?" Mother asks.

"She was *never* with Rob. She's getting married to somebody else."

Mother plops on the edge of the tub. "When did this come about?"

"She just called. I want to kill her. She's gone insane."

Mother scowls and chews on her lip. "Is there a baby involved?"

I nod yes.

"Is she sure about the father?"

"Yes!" I say, exasperated.

"Well, how should I know, Mary Margaret? From what I've observed, it's a legitimate question."

"She's not what you think!" I snap. "But she wants me there at city hall on Saturday. And I . . . I don't think I can."

"Well, at least *he's* stepping up," Mother says. "That's saying something for him. I wish the fellow great good luck, because with a girl like that, he's going to need it."

"That's cruel," I say.

"Yes, life can be cruel," Mother says. "Watch and learn."

The heat coming up my neck is making my itching

unbearable. "I don't want to talk about this with you anymore!" I shout, scratching furiously. "I'm sorry I even told you!"

She stands and opens the medicine cabinet, pulls out some hay fever pills. "These will help the hives," she says, slapping the box in my hand. "Take two."

"Lord have mercy," she says to the ceiling, and leaves.

24

$\mathcal{L}$ater I decide to call Mitch and tell him the whole story.

"How did they get Donnie to do it is what I want to know," I tell him. "I don't think he cares about her at all."

"The draft is a mighty good incentive," Mitch says. "Plus she's underage, her dad's a lawyer. . . ."

On Friday night, I will the phone to ring. Jane will either be in tears or laughing off the whole thing. But it will be over, and I can go back to breathing again.

Saturday morning dawns. "Were there any calls for me last night?" I ask Dad.

"Nope," he says.

I go out in bare feet to my secret garden and light up one of my mother's stolen cigarettes. Is there someone up there I can pray to? Who takes care of us bad girls, anyway?

At the sound of the whoosh of the sliding back door, I shrink behind a rosebush.

"Mary Margaret?" Mother calls.

I don't answer.

"I see you, for God's sake," she says. "Come on over here."

Shoot.

"And bring that cigarette," she says.

Mother sits on the lawn chair and directs me to do the same. She taps her own cigarette out of the box and lights it with a kitchen match. I don't know whether to just hold on to my Pall Mall or to inhale in front of her.

"So here we are, my dear," Mother says. "What are we going to do?"

"You mean about Jane?"

"Uh-huh." Mom crosses her legs and smokes. "You going to the church?"

"It's not going to be at a church, Mom."

"Well, wherever it is, I think you should go."

"You do? Why?"

"Because you should," says Mother. "It is a big deal. The biggest. And she's your friend, God help her."

I flick an ash and stare at the patio.

"Jane is a screwup and a very confused girl," Mother says. "She is also very young. Hopefully, this is going to be her only marriage, even if it's not in the church. So you should be there."

"It's in two hours," I say.

"Take a shower, put on a dress," Mother says. "I'll drive you."

"Really?"

"Yes."

I take a puff, blow a sidestream of smoke.

"You've been doing this for a long time, haven't you?" Mother asks.

"Just this last year," I say.

"Nasty habit," Mother says. She grabs my cigarette and stamps it out in her ashtray. "Go shower."

Before we get to the freeway, Mother turns into the Piggly Wiggly parking lot, stops in front of the Holland Bakery, and says, "You're bringing the cake."

"What? No, I'm not."

"A bride needs a cake."

"This is all no-frills, Mom. It's an unwedding wedding."

"Dear, there's no such thing."

"She won't want it."

"You stay here, then. I'm going to get a little cake, that's all. Say it's from you and me both."

The Holland Bakery is expensive. I watch Mom through the window picking out a small white cake with white roses. As she counts out the money from her old leather wallet, I wonder if she got a cake on her own rushed wedding day.

Mother returns, puts the box on my lap. "I made them put a wedding bell on top," she says. "Pretty, isn't it?"

"It looks nice, Mom." We listen to her radio station all the way to city hall. Some guy is singing about wanting to be

223

around to pick up the pieces when somebody breaks her heart. One after another, they're all romantic songs sung by old men.

"Do you know where to go?" Mother asks as we stop in front of the municipal building.

"I'll figure it out," I say.

"Want me to come?" she says.

"I'm okay," I say.

"Good," says Mother. She opens her coin purse and drops money in my bag. "For the bus ride home," she says, leaning over to kiss my cheek.

I start opening the door.

"Wait!" she says. She dabs at my cheek with Kleenex. "Lipstick."

"Thanks," I tell her. I stand and wave, watch her taillights disappear down the long street, then make my way to the marriage license room.

On the third floor, I spot a double door with stamped glass that says JUSTICE OF THE PEACE. Pushing it open, I get my first glimpse of the waiting-room crowd. There's a lady my mother's age dressed in lilac hanging on her fiancé's arm, a collegiate-looking couple, a mother-daughter team looking petrified. And then Mrs. Stephens. For this occasion, I'd expected her to be all moist and trembly. Instead, both she and Avery look like they're waiting for traffic court instead of a wedding.

As soon as she sees me, Barbara Stephens perks up. "Mary Margaret!" she croons. She takes the cake from me and, like the good hostess she is, thanks me over and over. "Jane is in the ladies' room," she says.

"Where's Donnie?"

"Getting some air, I'd imagine," she says carefully.

"Should I go get her?"

"Oh, would you?" says Mrs. Stephens. "She's just down the hall to the left."

It's twenty till eleven. Dread sweeps over me as I reach the bathroom. I count to three, then open the door.

Jane is wearing a billowy white smock dress with Mexican embroidery. Her hair is tied up with a strip of tanned leather. She's standing in front of the mirror, not putting on makeup or brushing her hair—just looking at herself. When she turns to me, she clasps her hands to her chest.

"You came! I knew you'd come!" she says.

I let her hug me. "You look pretty," I say. "As usual."

"I feel amazing," she says. "Not sick like they always say. And you know all that stuff about cravings? Well, I just crave *everything*." Her eyes are shiny, and her cheeks are a glowing coral. "I am so completely happy, Mary Margaret."

"Your mother wants you," I say.

"I'm sure she does," says Jane. "I don't have to come whenever she calls anymore, do I?"

"Guess not."

Jane holds me by the shoulders and backs me up. "You're not really happy for me, are you?"

"I want to be. Really."

Jane launches into an explanation of how I can't possibly understand and that's okay. Because this looks like a primitive shotgun wedding, but the actual marriage will be new and different and like nothing anyone's tried before.

"We're going to live at Donnie's at first. He and Richard are going to make jewelry. And then we're going to travel down the coast and sell it. Just sell enough to buy food and grass and the necessaries." She folds her arms. "We're not going to own a lot of shit."

"Where will you have the baby?" I ask.

"I'll let the baby decide that." Jane smiles.

"So the baby's in on it, too?"

"Yes," Jane says. "The baby's already chosen Donnie and me. And obviously, the baby doesn't want Donnie to go to Vietnam." She runs her hands over her belly. "If the baby knows how to save his daddy from the guns, he must be a wise little creature."

"We should probably go," I say.

Back in the waiting room, Donnie joins the Stephenses. He stands, expressionless, at an unsociable distance.

Donnie, I think, *keeping all still among the chaos, going all placidly among the noise and haste, blah, blah, blah. . . .* There's no one here to be best man. But then again, Avery probably scared everyone at the Rainbow House away.

Jane takes Donnie's arm and massages it. I see Donnie roll his shoulders slightly as if to break her grip.

The door to the inner chambers opens, and a grinning boy and girl come out. The girl throws her little bouquet of daisies in the air and yells, "Catch!"

226

Jane nabs the flowers in midair. "I love daisies," she says, holding them under her chin. And I just know she's taking this as another fabulous omen.

"Donald Horowitz and Jane Stephens," says a woman in a tweed suit.

"That's us!" squeals Jane.

We all file in. The man performing the ceremony welcomes us. He takes the marriage certificate that Mrs. Stephens has brought in a manila envelope. He has a severe summer cold and must stop several times to blow his nose.

We watch as the state of Oregon gives its blessing to the union of this man, Donald, and this woman, Jane. I notice that it makes them swear to commit their lives to each other but doesn't specifically require them to be in love.

When Jane repeats after the judge, she sounds like she's auditioning for a Shakespeare play. When Donnie says the same words, he sounds uncustomarily jittery.

"I now pronounce you man and wife," the judge says.

Each syllable stabs my heart. I think I'm going to need a tourniquet.

Jane stands on her toes and throws her arms around her husband for their kiss. There's a loud smacking sound. Mr. and Mrs. Stephens and I stand paralyzed.

"That's it!" says the judge. "That's all there is. Good luck."

Mr. Stephens takes his wife by the elbow and guides her toward the door.

This isn't right, I think. It's sad. No congratulations, no photographs. And then I remember my mother's cake.

I pick it up from where it rests on a folding chair. Mrs. Stephens blinks as if she just woke up.

"Jane," she says. "Mary Margaret brought a wedding cake. Would you like to go outside and cut it?"

"How sweet!" Jane says. "How perfect."

We find a little concrete table in the courtyard. I set the cake in the center, realizing I haven't brought a knife, forks, or plates. "I'm afraid I've come sort of unprepared," I say.

Jane reaches in and pulls out a chunk of cake with her hands. She offers a bit to Donnie, who nibbles, then she stuffs the rest in her own mouth.

She laughs and hungrily licks the icing off her fingers. It's like she's having a party all by herself.

"Please, everybody! Help yourselves!" Jane pinches off a bit more cake, which she offers me. "Open wide," she says.

I take the cake, feel the buttery frosting around my mouth, close, chew, choke, and swallow.

"Anyone else?" Jane says.

"Why don't you take it with you, darling?" says Mrs. Stephens.

Jane puts the cake back inside the box and hands it to Donnie. "I'll have my husband carry this for me," she says proudly.

Donnie and Jane are going back to Centralia. We follow them back to Donnie's orange van. Jane gives each of us extravagant hugs—even Avery gets one. Donnie hangs back, then makes for the driver's side.

I run after him. He stops and stares at me. I reach down,

take his hand, and squeeze. "Please . . . ," I say. That's all I can come up with.

"Peace," he says.

"Come visit!" Jane calls from the passenger's seat. "Promise!"

When they rumble off, I notice Jane doesn't look back.

"Would you like a ride home?" Avery asks.

"Me? No," I say. "Thank you for asking."

"Thank you for coming," Mrs. Stephens says briskly. "Thank you very much."

I start walking slowly, through the parking lot, down the street. I need to sit and think. Or better yet, sit and not think. Most of all, I want to be alone. So when I see the cathedral two blocks ahead, I decide it's as good a place as any to hide away.

The church has thick double doors made of wooden planks that swing open easily when I pull on the handles. My heels sound like hammer blows as I walk into the marble vestibule. I watch the streak of light, full of dancing dust, disappear when the doors thud shut.

I try a second set of doors, imagining that I will sit for a while with my private misery under the vaulted ceilings of a massive and empty church. Then I see that the pews are draped with ropes of pink roses—someone has decorated for an afternoon wedding.

At the end of the church, beyond the communion rail and to the left of the altar, stands a statue of blue-robed Mary. Her arms are open, as if to say, *Come to me!*

I sit myself down in the last row. How many girls in veils have walked down this aisle toward that embrace? I think of Jane, lured like a zombie.

"I am so mad," I say, closing my eyes. "And so afraid. I don't want to be alone again." I rest my head in my hands and press hard until I see stars.

When I was a kid, I'd beg my mother to let me drop a dime in the collection box so I could light a prayer candle and pay my respects to the Blessed Mother. I'd kneel and say what was in my heart and leave my burdens with her. It was a comforting thing to do, but I can't remember which I liked more: saying the prayer and feeling better or striking the match.

I stand and make my way down the aisle, no flowers, no veil. The Virgin hovers above the bank of flames. I kneel, take a dime from my bag and drop it in the collection box, strike a match, and light a candle in a ruby red cup. Then from somewhere comes a voice. It's not a voice you hear in your ears—but I'm certain that it's as real.

"Look up."

I look and see the candles twinkling at Our Lady's feet like a little city of wishes. And then I remember my dream.

"Your feet," I say. "I've found them."

When I look up at her from this angle, her arms seem to gesture downward. I know that every candle here represents someone's unanswered question or apology or plea for help.

"All this," she seems to say. "All the need and un-certainty that are bestowed upon me."

And I think, *Yes. Maybe she blesses them, too.*

Now I feel ready to go. Is it that I've found my own feet?

The summer afternoon light hurts my eyes, but I blink until I see clearly. Who knows when the next bus will arrive? I'll sit until one comes to take me home.

My home. Where the rooms will soon be even more crowded. Where my mother's moods will surely shift and storm. But even home can be a stop on the way to somewhere else.

Me, I'm staying free.

A Note From Kathy O'Dell

For me, one of the many pleasures of writing *Bad Tickets* was revisiting the pop songs of the 1960s. The early part of the decade featured swoony girls yearning for the boy of their dreams. Take a listen to "Where the Boys Are," a song made popular by Connie Francis:

> *Till he holds me, I wait impatiently.*
> *Where the boys are, where the boys are, someone waits*
> *for me. . . .*

Now compare those lyrics to "Different Drum," a song sung by the now-famous Linda Ronstadt when she was with the Stone Poneys.

> *All I'm saying is I'm not ready*
> *For any person, place, or thing*
> *To try and pull the reins in on me.*

Big difference, right? And a reflection of the changes going on in the world at that time.

In sum, perhaps no one said it more succinctly than Lennon and McCartney:

> *She's got a ticket to ride,*
> *And she don't care. . . .*

Have fun writing your own ticket. And happy traveling!